ROUSE FAMILY CHRISTMAS

A SAG HARBOR BLACK ROMANCES CHRISTMAS NOVELLA

LULA WHITE

Rouse Family Christmas novella is the <u>fifth</u> book in this series about romance, family and community in the Black Hamptons.

There is no character development or backstory in this fifth installment, and it is assumed the reader is acquainted with this world.

For readers who are unfamiliar, your experience may be enhanced by following the reading order below.

The events do not occur based on numeric sequence of the books:

Brown Sugar This Christmas

Hot Chocolate This Winter

Flinging All Spring

Overheated for Summer

One Tasty Night

Explore You

Rouse Family Christmas

Christmas Down Under (Web site only, not for sale)

Taste You

Drink You

See Through You

Find You

Books In The *Sag Harbor Black Romances*

Brown Sugar This Christmas - Maddy & Jerrell

Hot Chocolate This Winter - Chrissy & Sheldon Part 1

Flinging All Spring - Adella & Desmond

Overheated for Summer - Chrissy & Sheldon Part 2

Rouse Family Christmas - All Couples

Books in the *Explore Men of the Hamptons* series

One Tasty Night - Solomon & Chaitra

Explore You - Kevin & Cher

Christmas Down Under - Keenan & Eugenia

Taste You - Solomon & Chaitra

Drink You - Lion & Kamila

See Through You - Keenan & Eugenia

Find You - Roland & Neeraja

It all started with 3 childhood friends
Books 1-4

Maddy

Chrissy

Adella

The Old Hamptons Money

ELLIS/PAGE BLOODLINE

Maddy marries Jerrell
William
Marguerite

TOWNSEND COUSINS

Chrissy marries Sheldon
Cher marries Kevin
Neeraja marries Roland

ENGLISH FAMILY

Solomon marries Chaitra
Lonnie
Constance
Rachel
Martin
Adella marries Desmond
Ilyana

MIDDLETON SONS

Lion marries Kamila
Brendan
Kevin marries Cher

These Black families have thrived in New York since 1700s & 1800s.

The English family arrived in the 1970s & 80s during the real estate boom.

Explore Adventures is created by Keenan, Solomon, & Kevin

New Hamptons Money, Books 5-12

ROUSE FAMILY

Roland marries Neeraja
Sheldon married Chrissy
(ex-wife is Eugenia)
Etta
Kamila marries Lion
Jerrell marries Maddy

These Black families arrived in New York after 2000.

MCLAIN FAMILY

Chaitra marries Solomon
Desmond married Adella
Keenan loves Eugenia

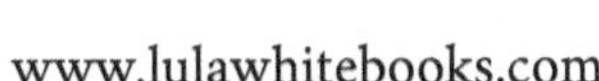

www.lulawhitebooks.com

email: lula@lulawhitebooks.com www.blackluxuryromances.com

ROUSE FAMILY CHRISTMAS
PLAYLIST

Hey Loves, I have a music playlist for most of the books in the series. These are the songs I listened to while writing this story. In my more intimate posts on Patreon, I'll share the songs I listened to on repeat and which songs defined some scenes.

On Spotify it's free to set up an account, open up the web player and listen for free. Here's Rouse Family Christmas on Spotify.

MADDY

𝐸laborate guests wrapped in furs and sequins, donning priceless, rare jewels, strutted down the red rope, filing into the building formerly known as the *Ivory*, for its first Christmas under new ownership.

Over their heads swung giant golden bells. Surrounding them were life-sized Black nutcrackers, and three-dimensional Black Christmas ballerinas dancing in a holographic display. A forest of white Christmas trees and snow formed a path toward the dining room.

Black residents from Nineva, Sag Harbor Hills, and Azurest, some of whom hadn't visited the Black Hamptons in years, *oohed* and *aahed* at the new decor, which had barely been installed only days before.

Chrissy, Adella and Maddy had worked with a design team to create an updated version of the Winter Wonderland that was reminiscent of their magical childhoods at the *Ivory*. Even though the friends owned it now, they would try and keep as many of Black Sag Harbor's old ways and traditions as possible, mixed with new flavor in the modern, swank furniture, lighting and fixtures.

"Oh, my God," Mrs. Page, Maddy's mother, gushed as her gaze wandered across all the baubles and gewgaws that glistened over the ground and track lights. "You ladies were not playing around, were you?"

"We wanted to make sure we kept to tradition and improved on it. What do you think?" Maddy whispered, while her own eyes danced at all the hard work the crews had put in.

The treasures at which they all gazed now had been months in the making, since she and her friends had earned their big victory over their number one enemy. Numerous trips Maddy had taken from her Capitol Hill job in D.C., to Sag Harbor to ensure every fixture and piece of furniture was situated to deliver a digitized, three-dimensional experience. With the help of Sheldon's technological hand, of course. So *Dream Stage* could indeed be dream-like.

"Breathtaking. As is everything you do," Mrs. Page mused, squeezing her oldest daughter tighter to her.

"As if her head needs to get any bigger," Maddy's brother, William, said behind her, giving his big sister's hip a push. But he also beamed from ear to ear while his attention danced from one spectacle to another.

Right behind them walked the Rouse family. Jerrell Rouse held his and Maddy's son Chase, who wasn't yet three months old.

"Y'all could've taken all this money and put it into some condos," an older voice joked. It was Maddy's father-in-law, the patriarch of the Rouse clan, Charles Rouse.

"I could've taken this money down to the casinos in Nawlins, gotten me some dancing girls and a purple pimp suit." Roland Rouse, the oldest of Jerrell's siblings, joined in the wise cracks.

"You wouldn't have had a wife and family to come back to," his wife, Princess, responded with quickness.

The entire group laughed as both families all stopped on the step-and-repeat to pose for photos as a group.

Maddy rolled her eyes at both men. "Thank God there are people like Princess and me in the world to lead you sheep when you go astray."

"That's right, daughters-in-law, give it to 'em," Jerrell's mother, Professor Verona Rouse, added while they still posed for the photographers.

"When do we get to the part where I eat my grandmama's cooking?" Sheldon Rouse cracked. "That's the only reason I came."

"Oh, really? That's the only reason, huh?" asked his fiancée Chriselle, who was headlining the event. "We'll see if that's your story when we get home tonight."

"Ooohhhh," the families crowed while busting up with laughter and rubbing Sheldon's bald head.

But just as Sheldon had pointed out, their family matriarch, Pauletta Rouse, had the entire restaurant smelling like a baked heaven. Even from the front foyer, whiffs of southern hot delectables teased their growling stomachs. Desserts and savory stuffed goodies they'd grown up eating down in Louisiana, now excited the guests' nostrils —Pauletta's Pecan Fire, Red Velvet Heaven, Sweet Potato Creams and Bourbons from the Boot.

After photos, Maddy and Chrissy moved to the front of the dining room, where they were joined by their childhood friend, Adella McClain. All three women now stood as business partners, in their triumphant resurrection of the *Ivory*.

As they linked arms, the entire room of Black Hamptons *Who's Who*, joined by well-wishers of other races and cultures, stood to clap until the roof thundered. All for the grand re-opening of one of the most historic Black establishments in America.

Once they'd taken photos for the *New England Standard*, the *Wall Street Chronicle*, *Hollywood Tattler*, and other national newspapers and magazines, Maddy and Adella took their seats at the side of the stage.

Their friend Chriselle took center stage.

"Hi, Mommy!" her daughter Kara called out from where she sat in Sheldon Rouse's arms. "Do a good job and I'll give you a cookie, okay?"

The audience broke into laughter as Chrissy's face brightened at the sound of her daughter's voice.

"Hi, Baby," Chrissy gushed from the stage. "I'll try my best. You know how I love Grandma Pauletta's cookies." She turned to the musician leader and gave a quick nod.

What a difference a year makes, Maddy thought to herself at this sight.

The last time they were all gathered here for Christmas, complete and utter chaos had unfolded between Chrissy and her now ex-husband, with their son Blake throwing fits. Then, with the year of bidding wars and betrayals between Maddy and her childhood enemies, they'd almost lost this precious piece of Black history.

Now, as Chrissy sang Celine Dion's rendition of *O, Holy Night*, the stars truly did appear to be brightly shining again in Sag Harbor.

Finally.

Southampton's Episcopalian Church Choir moved into the stands, led by children, all carrying fake candles. Maddy and Adella held hands and wiped the shared emotion welling up in their eyes. They began to sing the chorus backing Chrissy up. Not a single other sound or movement disturbed the room.

As Maddy's heart filled up with all the love and preciousness in that song, she stared toward the center of the dining room, at her new husband and baby. The last few weeks had been rough for them. Ever since that fateful October day, when she'd received an ominous visit.

Since then, she and Jerrell had been trying their hardest to work through the fallout.

When Maddy's eyes rested on the loves of her life, Jerrell was already staring back at her.

I love you, she mouthed.

A moment passed. Even in the dim lighting, she might have sworn she saw his face flinch. Perhaps a flicker of pain darkened his eye. But nevertheless, he managed to mouth back, *I love you.*

His hesitation emphasized the new wall between them. She batted back tears, returning her attention to her long-time friend, Chriselle, who was singing her heart out.

"You all right?" Adella whispered, pressing life back into Maddy's arm.

Maddy gave a slight nod. "Barely."

After the opening song, a peaceful glow fell across the room of entranced attendees.

Pastor Arnold came to give the opening prayer and remarks.

"We couldn't be more proud of these ladies and this community for coming together in such a loving and glorious way. The *Ivory* has been through so much this year, but we never doubted for a moment that the strong arm of the Lord would pull us through. And hold us all together."

"Amen," many attendees called out from the audience.

"Will every head bow and every spirit reflect?" Pastor Arnold said. But before the Pastor's head dropped, his eyes shot to the back of the room. "Oh, what a blessing we have with us tonight. Praise God. Come on in, young brothers."

Every head in the dining room turned to the entrance at the top of the stairs. Hushed murmurs swept across the audience.

Maddy and Chrissy swapped stares of silent resentment.

"The nerve of them to come here," Adella muttered.

Maddy fought to appear unaffected. But on the inside, she was seeing red, and not from the decorations. She couldn't believe they had the audacity. As well as the gall of the woman who now stood alongside them.

Standing at the doorway was Solomon. Martin. Keenan. And Kevin. At his side, her arm nestled comfortably inside his, stood Chrissy's cousin Cher.

This time, when Maddy's gaze tripped back to her husband, no love could be found anywhere on Jerrell's face as he glared at her, and then cut his gaze away…

To the man who stood between them.

"WHAT ARE YOU DOING HERE? How *dare* you show your faces when you were *not* invited," Maddy hissed at Kevin after she'd strutted down the aisle and slipped behind the Christmas trees. Now, she moved only her lips.

Kevin's piercing eyes now pierced her.

"You might be the owner of the *Ivory* now, Maddy—"

"Dream. Stage. It is *Dream Stage*," she returned.

"And regardless of its ownership, it is *still* a piece of history that belongs to us *all*. Not just you," he answered.

"Maddy, we only came to support this place," Cher chimed in. "We all grew up in this building, just like you did. Come on. Don't act like this."

Maddy ignored Cher and focused her ire on the man she'd once thought was the man of her dreams. Throughout this entire year, he'd only brought nightmares. Especially to her brand-new marriage in the last few weeks.

She stared around, at him and all his business partners with whom she'd warred over the last few months. "I couldn't tell from all the magazine and television interviews where you put us down and questioned if we could bring this place back from the ashes."

"But you did it," Adella's brother, Solomon, said. "And now we're here to salute you."

"That's right," Desmond McClain's brother, Keenan, added. "You did it. All the competition and bluster set aside, job well done."

Kevin's set jaw and probing stare twisted right into her insides, while the two of them reopened their lifelong conversation. He always seemed to get the best of her. To shut off her defenses, freeze her thoughts, and trap her in a maze of helplessness. No matter how smart Maddy had always been, he'd always been smarter.

And now, in his latest form of torture, he'd dragged her into her deepest hole from which Maddy was unsure she could ever escape.

"What's going on out here?" Unsure, irritated, her husband's voice asked her so much more than that one question. Jerrell appeared carrying a wide-eyed Chase, whose eyes found his mother's. Both father and son studied her as if questioning her in the same way.

"I was just asking these men who invited them." Maddy inhaled.

"Me," another voice said from the entrance to the foyer. "It was me. I invited them to come and be part of this celebration, which is a *community* gathering, and not simply business or proprietary. Or at least it shouldn't be," Pastor Arnold explained, stepping toward all of them. "Now, look, everybody. We just went over all this a couple months ago. And the very same weekend that we promised to do better, you all went right back to betraying and humiliating one another."

"Or at least one of us did the betraying," Kevin muttered, shooting his glare straight into Maddy's conscience.

"I was hoping while everyone was in town, we could all talk. About starting a Black Business Council here on the East End. So *all* of you can make a concerted effort to move in lock step with one another next year."

"I have no problem with that, Pastor," Kevin responded.

"Me neither," Keenan added.

The Pastor peered at Maddy over the rim of his glasses. "The other Black business-owners have already offered their cooperation. All, but you and Jerrell."

Maddy knew Kevin was only appearing to be conciliatory because Pastor Arnold was present. As soon as he got the chance, Kevin would be right back to his scheming, underhanded ways. After that weekend in the Catskills, when he'd come to her family's home, he'd deliberately thrown a hand grenade into her marriage.

"I have to be honest, Pastor. I don't trust Mr. Middleton, and I'll have to think about it."

"Madison," Pastor Arnold pressed, "please don't tell me that you, Del, and Chrissy went to all this trouble of saving the *Ivory*, so you could start using your influence to divide us. This place was supposed to keep us together. I hope we can still count on you to lead us in that."

With no further words, Maddy stepped aside. Kevin and the others walked into the entrance.

Once the pastor and the guys made their exit, Jerrell turned to her, as Sheldon, Desmond and Adella filed in.

"Did you know he would be here?" Jerrell asked under his breath.

"Do I look like I knew?" she shot back.

He sucked his teeth, bearing down on his wife with a hard glare. "If your old boyfriend has taught us anything, it's that looks can be deceiving, can't they?"

I CAN'T UNHEAR THAT

SHELDON & CHRISSY

SHELDON

"**C**ome on down, baby, take a seat," Sheldon murmured, stepping onto the stage. He turned to all the musicians. "Everybody, take ten. Thanks."

"Shel, no, I need to work through this set and be ready to—"

"Chriselle," Sheldon interrupted, quieting his fiancée. He knew he needed to keep her calm, this month of all months. He slid his arms around her pregnant waist. "Chris..." He breathed. "Chrissy, I said take a seat. We agreed the only way you would do *two* shows in *one* weekend was if you took rest breaks every hour and only rehearsed three hours a day at this point in the pregnancy. Now, if you're not going to abide by that, I'm pulling rank and vetoing this performance, baby."

He saw the stress and tension all over her, and was trying the best he could to manage it. In addition to handling his own.

Rolling her eyes, Chrissy set the music sheets down. Sheldon's arms were waiting for her when she sat on his lap. Both their hands massaged her burgeoning belly. Outside of *MAC Dream Stage*, a light snow was beginning to fall on the Sag Harbor streets.

Chrissy's eyes fell to their hands intertwined with one another. "I can't stop thinking about the two of them standing there together last night. Her fawning all over him. She didn't even sit with her family. She sat with *his*."

If Chrissy loved anything in this world, it was her cousins, Cher and Neera.

"Can you blame her? You and Maddy practically kicked her out of yours," he murmured back, making sure to keep his voice soft, and his numerous worries and doubts in check.

"I still don't understand why you did that, Shel."

He leaned his chin against her shoulder. "You know why. Cher's a grown woman now, not some toddler you need to protect. She's not you. You can't keep projecting your past mistakes onto her, out of fear she'll do what you did. That girl—*woman*—has carried herself well as an adult. No hurtful relationships, no missteps with her money or career. All she's ever done is what you all expected, and she's thrived, Chris."

"That won't last with Kevin. He'll hurt her." Her face scrunched into a fist. "He's a hurtful jackass."

Sheldon eased his hands over his fiancée to calm her, and partly to calm himself. "If that happens, you'll be there to help her pick up the pieces. But in the short time I've known her, I've never seen her light up the way she did the other night." He buried his face in her arm. "You've got a performance tonight, and that should be your focus. So, Chriselle, what's this really about?"

He had a feeling that Chriselle knew but couldn't bring herself to say. Her silence formed the source of his fear.

Finally, she whispered, "Why can't we just be rid of him?"

Before he could answer, footsteps turned them to the entrance. Where a stranger stood, walking slowly toward them. "Happy Holidays, folks. I'm looking for a," the gentleman started, pausing to check his large, manila envelope. "Chriselle Townsend?"

In Shel's arms, Chrissy's muscles stiffened.

"I'm her."

The courier handed her the envelope. "You're being served, ma'am. By Mr. Blake Mason."

Both she and Sheldon scoffed. "Figures. Of course, I am."

Her trembling fingers opened the envelope, and she and Sheldon skimmed over two motions. Her ex-husband was seeking to terminate spousal alimony and support in light of her pregnancy and pending marriage to Sheldon, requesting to lift the monitor for his visits with his children for the holidays, and to terminate the five-year restraining order she had against him.

"We'll take care of it, like we always do. This is nothing." Sheldon squeezed her shoulders. The musicians started to come back from break.

Behind them was Maddy, with Jerrell not far behind. In his arms was their two-and-half month-old son, Chase.

"Ho ho ho," Jerrell called. "We all ready to go?"

Sheldon snickered as he and his younger brother went in for a grip. "Dude, your rhyming skills are—"

"Dope?" Jerrell asked.

"Corny," Sheldon answered, taking his little nephew into his arms. "Chase here can probably come up with better rhymes and he can't even talk yet. Isn't that right, little man? Tell your daddy he needs to stick with pastry sales."

After Maddy greeted Sheldon, she made her way to Chrissy.

"Hey, Boo. You look like you're getting snowed under,

girl. How's it going? You sure you can still do this tomorrow? Don't forget we have Tennessee ready in case you need to rest."

Sheldon couldn't help noticing how Chrissy practically melted into Maddy, both of them grabbing one another for dear life. He watched the two old friends communicate in silence.

They were clearly sharing all the frustration and fury they dare not speak aloud to Sheldon and Jerrell.

CHRISSY

Although Chrissy loved Sheldon with everything in her, and her fiancé was indeed her best friend, there was no one else on the planet who could truly understand Chrissy's humiliation, except Maddy.

Right now, there was no greater relief than the presence of her childhood running buddy in the Hamptons.

Chrissy's lips mumbled low so only Maddy heard it. "I'm just glad you showed up when you did."

The tension couldn't get any thicker, and the men seemed to sense Chrissy and Maddy needed a moment.

"Ay, fellas, why don't we all just take a long lunch?" Sheldon called to the band. He turned toward Chrissy with eyes of understanding.

On second thought, she couldn't decipher if they were

understanding, or actually accusing. Was her husband-to-be tweaked that she was confiding in Maddy what she still couldn't quite articulate to him?

Sheldon swallowed. "Sweetheart, Jerrell and I are going to take the baby and..." He scratched his head. "I don't know. Escape, maybe."

Chrissy noticed Jerrell and Maddy exchange tense expressions. Normally, he would go to Maddy for a kiss and a wisecrack before they went their separate ways.

Not this time.

Instead, the brothers held their own tiny exchange before heading out through the beautiful white wintry decor that did not match their current mood.

"Ever since that meeting, do you feel like Satan?" Chrissy asked.

Maddy stopped biting down on her bottom lip long enough to answer. "Worse."

"Have you tried talking to him?" Chrissy asked.

Maddy rolled her eyes. "Too many times to count. He can't get past it. He lies next to me at night all stiff like I'm some stranger he doesn't know anymore." Plopping into a chair, she rubbed her forehead. "The doctor finally cleared us to have sex now after the baby, and he hasn't... touched..." Maddy's voice broke. "I wish I could go back to college all over again, just so I could undo it."

Chrissy scooted her chair closer to Maddy's so the two could connect. The thoughts Chrissy had been walling up in her conscious, she finally released. "I wish we could go back to childhood and push that Negro off a cliff."

They broke into chuckles.

"You don't mean that."

"Yes, I do," Chrissy declared.

"We tried everything we could. Kevin's not going anywhere. And we can't just ignore him." Maddy pulled out tissues and wiped her face, shooting a loaded stare at Chrissy.

Chrissy thought of her precious cousin, Cher. Who had gone and fallen in love with the jerk who'd caused them all so much pain. Their number one enemy.

"No, we can't ignore him, not anymore."

SHELDON

"No matter how many times I try, I can't *unhear* that shit, man." Jerrell's head fell while he confided in his big brother. "Who did I marry? What else has she done that I don't know about? What is she capable of? I didn't exactly think Maddy was a nun, but I did believe she was a strait-laced girl, who was smart enough to get a job with her brains and not her p—"

"Alright, man, stop. Just... bring it down a couple notches." Sheldon cuddled little Chase. "If you haven't let her talk to you about it, then you don't know the whole story, and you're just getting caught up in your own head."

"She *fucked* her college professor for a *job*. A job she led me to believe she got on her *own*." The words snow-blowed through Jerrell's clenched teeth. "And Middleton knew about it, like he's God." Now he clenched his fists. "End of story. There's nothing else to talk about."

Jerrell spun out to lean against the door, facing Main Street.

"Don't you wonder how much more that dude knows about Chriselle? What other secrets he has on them that they haven't told us? How *he* knows them better than *we* do?" The youngest Rouse man pounded his chest. "It's almost like these damn Sag Harbor kids are some kind of broken up gang or something. On some love-hate BS."

Sheldon cooed the baby so Chase wouldn't get worked up from the anger in his father's voice. "Sure, I do. But then I remember my girl is six months pregnant, and for the sake of our unborn daughter and our children, I have to play it cool. Not get her too upset."

Jerrell shuddered, though ample heat blew through the vents. Sheldon watched him disappear inside his thoughts. "You should have seen how smug that dude looked. Sitting there with his expensive threads, rolling up in a chauffeured truck with security, chest all out, laying into my wife. My *wife!*" The words torpedoed through his clenched teeth, before his open palm banged the glass.

Only once he heard his baby boy whimper behind him did Jerrell stop and take a breath. "It's my job to protect her. But there wasn't shit I could do for her then. Except sit there. And watch him have this... *power* over her. While they've got this energy, between just the two of them. Which I have no clue where it starts." He fumed and pivoted back to Sheldon, "or where it ends. You don't know how weak I felt. Like that dude's got my nuts in his hands."

Sheldon sniffed. "I think I do, man. Don't forget, Genie had mine in her hands for three years after she left and took my kid with her."

The door to the restaurant swung open, and in stepped Adella and Desmond.

"My folks!" Desmond threw up his arms. "What's good?"

"Gentlemen, hello there, how are New York's finest daddies?" Adella said, exchanging hugs with the brothers.

"Never better," Sheldon replied with a forced smile.

"Uh oh. What's that about?" Adella noted. "My girls are still doing alright, aren't they?"

Sheldon exchanged stares with Jerrell, before the younger brother replied, "Sure, they're alright. I'm not too sure about the rest of us."

"Aw, hell," Desmond added. "Something's up. Man, you can't ever hide your attitude. We can always see it like a neon sign in a dump truck."

"Well, well, guess what? Your little stinkpot here just took a nice dump in Uncle Shelly's arms and needs to be changed. Time for Daddy Duty, man." Sheldon started to hand Chase back to his father when Adella stepped up.

"I'll take Chase, and we'll head to the dining room with his mom," she said, throwing Desmond a suspicious look that Sheldon wondered about. "That way, you gentlemen can talk."

"Talk?" Sheldon and Jerrell asked at the same time.

Adella smiled a little too sweetly. "Mmhm. Talk."

Desmond turned to the others. Pinched the bridge of his nose with his fingers, before his lips curled in. "Drinks, fellas?"

They stared back at him.

Thirty minutes later, they sat at *Bottoms Up*, a bar situated a few doors down.

"No." Jerrell's voice couldn't have been flatter than dry concrete. "Who asked for this?"

"Keenan is asking for this," Desmond replied. "He's making an effort to pull Solomon and Adella together. It might take time, but they made a start over Thanksgiving."

"I suppose it's up to these women. They run every damn thing anyway," Jerrell muttered, before taking a long sip of brandy.

Sheldon inhaled. "Come on, J. The man has a point. There are not too many Black-owned businesses in the Hamptons. You all can't keep going on with this rivalry thing."

"And Keenan wants Poppin' Pauletta's to be there too." Desmond's chest swelled with the huge breath he took.

"Since Keenan's got a big wish list, why didn't he come and ask for all this himself?" Jerrell shot.

Desmond snickered. "Because Negro, would *you* come and ask you for something if you were anybody else but you right now? For nearly two months, you've been walking around scowling. Who wants to ask you something?"

Sheldon accidentally snorted his cognac while laughing. "Preach."

Jerrell sucked his teeth. "Is old boy going to be there?"

"Who?" Desmond asked.

Maddy's husband squinted. "You know who."

Desmond shrugged. "Does it matter? Business needs to be handled. Either way."

"No. I don't care what Maddy does with her company. But that's the answer from mine." Jerrell chucked back the rest of his liquor. Slammed down the glass. "It's like I can't escape this shit. What did I get myself into, marrying this damn girl?"

NOT A PROBLEM

ADELLA

That evening, a tired Adella entered her family's Hamptons compound after Chrissy's second performance. A few other extended relatives made their way to their rooms, while she and Desmond played host and exchanged pleasantries.

Though he wore a tense smile, Desmond only said as much as necessary. She could see he was itching to break free of the pretenses that came with greeting her family.

"How did it go with Jerrell?" Adella asked to break the slight awkwardness, as they made their way up the stairs.

Desmond shook his head. "He is at a hard no. If Kevin Middleton comes anywhere near this Black Business Council, J's out." He filled his lungs with oxygen as he helped Del out of her gown.

"And Pastor Arnold and the elders are putting pressure on *Dream Stage* to come to the table. We can't say no, or the girls and I look like jerks. Poor Maddy. She's stuck between a rock and a hard place."

Yet again, Adella's husband seemed to disappear to some place else in his head while he yanked on his silk pajama bottoms.

"Babe?" she called. "Nobody said anything crazy to you tonight, did they? The weekend's been going well for you, so far?"

Whenever they visited the Hamptons and attended these high-society events, Adella knew it made Desmond nervous. Even in his role as her husband, New York's polite society still wasn't his scene.

She was grateful that Jerrell had taken him in and opened some social doors. But it was clear in her man's bundled muscles and tight smile that Desmond felt out of place. Especially when people asked him what he was doing career-wise, now that he no longer played football or worked regularly at his mother's construction company. Though he was working at a brewery back in Boston, getting his MBA, and learning the ropes of business, he had no high-ranking title or responsibilities that garnered respect among cliques and elites who were obsessed with status.

"Nah, Baby," he replied. "Weekend was awesome, and you shined like the jewel you are."

His half-grin didn't reach his eyes. He wasn't telling her the truth, and eventually, she would have to wring it out of him.

For now, Del reached for a lace nightie, while he went through his nightly routine of brushing and flossing. He would need a little distraction.

When she finished her own routine, she stood and waited for him at the foot of the bed. "Why don't you show your jewel how priceless she is?"

His wet lips were smacking on her shoulder before she could lift her finger to beckon him.

"Not a problem," he whispered in her ear.

He teased the silk fabric over her nipple. Electric currents in Del's heart shot through the rest of her. The strap of her gown fell off at the command of his index finger. Goosebumps on her neck relished his tongue, where he stopped to nibble her ear.

Already, her nectar trickled down her thighs, smacking of wet anticipation. Desmond's hand mashed her whole breast, and the ecstasy dropped her jaw. Out slid her tongue.

"Give it to me," he commanded.

It took no time for her to lean into his mouth, offering her tongue that her husband devoured.

While his other hand slid between her thighs.

"Aaah," Adella whined, trying to control her noises since there were relatives in the house.

But her man made it so damn hard. Desmond sucked her tongue, while three of his fingers ignited her dripping womanhood. Over and over. Until she bucked.

Clamping her head to his, he prevented her from squirming or backing away, forcing her to endure the glorious torment of his fingers stroking her hot pussy walls. The more he annihilated her G spot, the more Del dripped. Since she couldn't scream or move, his wife could only lay her head on his shoulder and whimper.

The orgasm cooked in her womb, frying and popping in the fire of his insistent stroking. To withstand the out-of-body trip, she dug her nails into his upper back. Del's lungs took rugged breaths. The orgasm thundered underneath her belly button and down to her knees, buckling them.

Desmond picked her up and placed her in bed. With her juices still shining on all three of his fingers, he stuck them in his mouth and sucked them clean.

A spent Del pulled him down to her, and explored her husband's chest, abdomen, and between his legs until she met him at full attention. She clutched his desire.

Pulling out his dick, she slinked downward, until she lay underneath him. His erection longer than her face now, she opened her mouth. With pleasure, she watched his pupils hit his eyelids, when she inserted him as far as he would go. Desmond started stroking his length on her tongue. Del clutched the base of his dick and massaging his balls. It drove him nuts, and his face winced.

"Your lips are so fucking pretty around my dick, Baby," Desmond nearly whined while Del's head bobbed on his shaft. She collected more spit around her mouth to give him more slippage. He wrapped his big hand around hers, and they both pressed as he pumped against her tongue. He pulled out some to let her breathe, and she sucked and licked his head, using her tongue to smear his pre-cum around his tip. "Fuck."

Now he tried suppressing his glee. "I'm com… Hah…"

Warm seeds squirted into her throat, as she stared up at him. Desmond gripped her hair, and returned her gaze.

Not bothering to remove his pajamas that were still around his calves, he pushed her down onto the bed. Pressed his erection at her threshold. "Shit, you're so wet. I couldn't wait for today to be over so we could get to this part."

At the glory of feeling him fill her up, Adella arched her back and strapped her thighs to his. He lifted one of them up, before placing her foot on his shoulder, and the deeper penetration ripped through her womb. More of her cream trickled all over him. The strokes were too sweet and hot, until neither could hardly move.

Desmond groaned. Adella clung to his ass, pulling him into her while he punished her favorite corner.

"Damn," he squeaked.

Adella kept rolling her pelvis with his until their pelvises collided in unison. Stroking and jerking, they swayed together. Before his mouth crushed hers again. "I love you, baby."

"I love you," she said before he had finished his

sentence. Still connected and wrapped inside each other, they submerged in the sheets.

Moments later, as he began to snore, she said a silent prayer to God and her grandparents in heaven, that she had gotten pregnant this time.

ANYWHERE BUT HERE

MADDY

That night, Maddy and Jerrell returned to his Sag Harbor townhome. With her bones dragging, she packed her things and the baby's things to return to Washington, D.C., early the next morning.

"What are you thinking?" She asked him, standing across the bedroom.

"I'm not thinking. Thinking is the last thing I want to do," he replied.

She dropped in the clothes she was shoving into a suitcase and moved around the bed to where he undressed.

Maddy ran her hands over his tense back and wedged her face against his back muscles. "Tell me what to do. You and Chase mean more than anything to me. I don't want us going on like this. So, tell me what you want, and I'll do it."

Jerrell picked up both Maddy's hands and kissed them, and studied her face. All she wanted was to clear this mess that had divided them these past few weeks.

"Baby, I have to be honest, I don't know. I'm trying to forget. I swear I am."

"What Kevin said, it didn't mean anything to—"

"Don't. You could be telling me the truth. But I'll never know. You're going to say whatever sounds good, so you come out of this white as snow, the way you always do."

His words knifed Maddy. "How could you say that? It was ten years ago. Let it go."

Jerrell seethed. "You lied to me. Less than a year ago."

She combed her hands over her face and hair. Seeing the distrust and hurt in his eyes was eating at her. And in a few precious hours, she would have to leave and go back to D.C. with this chasm between them. The commute between New York and D.C. was taking its toll, getting harder for her to make. "I did not lie. I already had the job. I showed you. What else do you want me to do?"

Jerrell stared into her the way somebody would a

stranger. Like he was gathering every shred of his manhood just to face her.

Like any other time since their love started, her body responded to his nearness the way ice responded under heat. Her hands cupped his pecs, rubbed their firmness. Her nipples awaited Jerrell's hot tongue and hungry bites. This time, she only got his hands at the temples of her head.

"Why is it whenever things are good for us, that dude shows up and pulls your cord? Like you're his puppet? And he can control you, yank you, any way he wants."

Jerrell's eyes searched hers.

Maddy's fingers clung to his chest. "I'm looking at the man who controls every part of me."

Jerrell shook his head. "If that was true, why were you so upset when he walked in with Cher? That must've hurt, huh? Seeing him finally commit to somebody who's not you."

Maddy rolled her eyes, stung at the taunting way he said it. Cher being with Kevin didn't bother her at all. Instead, she was annoyed at his audacity of crashing hers and her friends' big night. Kevin had made the event about him, as always.

"I was not upset about him." She tried to pull away again, but Jerrell held on. "I was *not*! When will you stop punishing me just for knowing him?"

"When you stop looking at him like a little puppy who misses its true owner."

"Everybody was looking at them! Let go of me. You are such an asshole."

Jerrell flinched. "Me? Asshole? Or is the real asshole the

woman who led me to believe she's somebody she's not? And then of all the people on Earth who informs me of what you did, of how you really came up, it just had to be *him.* Is the real asshole the person who pretends she's some smart, self-sufficient diva when really all she is is a hoe?"

Quick as a thunder crack, Maddy's hand fired into his cheek.

"Whatever you *think* you see, it's your own damn jealousy!"

She snatched her son out of his arms. Chase woke up and started to wail.

Immediately, the door flew open and in burst Chriselle. "Just let me get the baby. He shouldn't be around if you two are doing this." She rushed toward Chase.

Sheldon was right behind her, coming to stand between Maddy and Jerrell.

"Get off me, man," Jerrell said, marching out of the bedroom.

"Where are you going?" Shel asked.

"I don't know. Anywhere but here."

"You need to take your wife and son to the airport in the morning," Sheldon called.

"She's so good at making shit happen. Let her figure out how to get to the airport. She doesn't need me."

Maddy inhaled her despair, unable to exhale it.

"Let him go. He's right. I don't need him."

THE NEXT MORNING, Maddy hauled herself out of Sheldon's Escalade and prepared mentally for the return to Capitol Hill. Stepping into brutal winter winds at seven in the morning, she stared at hers and Jerrell's little son, still sleeping in his car seat. And then tossed a glance over her shoulder at her beloved Sag Harbor, where her fondest moments had shaped her life.

She would force herself back onto that plane. But as hard as she tried to put on her game face, her mental armor no longer fit. This time, the Capitol Hill mover and shaker was no longer forcing just herself. She was forcing her family.

Sheldon whipped out the baby's stroller, and firmly secured the car seat into the grips, shaking and checking to make sure it locked.

While bracing herself for a rough day, she was surprised to feel her brother-in-law's arms encircle her shoulders.

He turned her around, until she faced him. "Come here, Little Sis."

Maddy's strength slipped from her superwoman deposit account. She crumbled against Sheldon. "It'll be okay. He'll be fine. He's just processing it."

"I'm not what he says I am, and it didn't happen the way he thinks it did. Damn Kevin Middleton!" Maddy cried on Sheldon.

Sheldon tightened his embrace of her. "Just chill and stay focused for my nephew. I'll talk to J.

Boarding the jet, and strapping into first class, this trip did not feel as purposeful as it once did, even a few months ago. Landing at Reagan International Airport, she shoved her little son's stroller through the terminal. While she lugged their bags with one arm, his diaper bag and her leather laptop carrier banged on her hip. After waiting five minutes for an elevator and maneuvering through the crowds, she finally jumped into the chauffeured car that awaited her and Chase.

She dropped the baby off at her brownstone with the nanny, before heading to the Dirksen Senate Office Building.

Even the vibe among her colleagues had changed over the past year. Since she had opened *MAC Dream Stage* with Chrissy and Adella, some of her Senate colleagues had become distant.

Maddy had always moved well in social circles, primarily by hiding her lineage and her Hampton's connections.

She had downplayed her wealth, that she had summered with some presidents' grandkids at Martha's Vineyard and Cape Cod, that her savings and retirement accounts amounted to more than some of them would see in their lifetimes. By hiding her opportunities and access to privilege, Maddy had earned the respect of her co-workers with her hard work, pure and simple. Most of them had no clue what occurred in the Hamptons.

But her secret life was blown wide open once she decided to support her friend Chriselle. They had opened a high-profile entertainment company. With all the press coverage she and Chrissy had gotten in the past few months, particularly for their rivalry with Kevin, Maddy's privilege had been blasted right into the open.

It was unavoidable. And her success had changed

people's attitudes toward her.

"Must be nice to roll in at 11:15, just a few minutes before lunch," one of the Legislative Assistants snickered from their desk.

Never mind that Maddy often took her laptop and work everywhere with her. That sometimes Jerrell would remove her phone or computer from her as she slept. That she had worked through most of her pregnancy, and even banged out some memos and legislative briefs to the Senator during her family leave while she should have been bonding with Chase. Never mind that, between *Dream Stage* negotiations and securing talent, funding, and sponsorships, she was double-fisting her cell phones and reading messages from Capitol Hill.

Each time one of her colleagues contacted her privately, on her personal phone, because they had an issue, she always took their calls. When most people were out club-bing, or dining, or hitting the political happy hours, she was reviewing and analyzing reports.

No, none of that mattered.

All that her colleagues saw now, no matter how much work Maddy put in, was that she was a privileged girl whose family summered in the Hamptons.

Winded from hustling through the building, she now plopped down at her desk that was crammed in a corner, where someone else had apparently sat earlier and left their coffee.

Why was she still here in a government job?

Several lobbying firms had offered triple her current salary. Companies and corporations had contacted Maddy for her logistical prowess, for the way she'd managed

Chrissy's singing debut while she was still working a full-time job. Maddy had also earned respect in media circles for coordinating Del's press operation when Del had spontaneously performed heart surgery on a boat.

Sheldon's bank had tried to court her several times, offering lobbying roles and Community Relations Vice President. News stations and networks had invited Maddy to guest anchor and become a political correspondent. Showrunners and producers called Maddy a natural. In the corporate sector, she could make three to four times the money she was making now. Not that she needed it, but need wasn't the point.

Now with a family, where would she get the most value for what had become her limited time?

She had been working to prove herself for nearly eight years in the name of getting a plum White House appointment, maybe chief domestic policy advisor or Secretary of Labor or eventually, White House Chief of Staff.

There was a time when she first arrived on the Hill, that she wanted to save the world.

Now, she only wanted to savor her son. Her most important position was as his mom. To see him smile, feel his little body wiggle in her arms so she could nuzzle him back to sleep.

And yes, she longed to quiet this chaos between her and the only asshole who owned her heart.

Walking past the soured faces and whispers of her coworkers, Maddy no longer wanted to save the world. Or rather, saving the world had fallen from her top priorities.

So, why was she enduring this office pettiness? What was she still working so hard to prove?

ANYTHING

SHELDON

After dropping off Maddy, Sheldon returned to his job in the city, intending to meet up with Jerrell later. He only hoped his little brother wasn't doing something stupid. Chrissy had stayed behind in Sag Harbor to handle some *Dream Stage* agreements and logistics for upcoming performances. Jerrell would bring her back to the city with him the next day.

Sheldon stopped a few blocks from his office in Manhattan to pick up coffee. The day hadn't even started, and he was already wound up. December winds whipped through his wool coat and crept inside his slacks, almost the way turmoil was sneaking into his family.

He understood precisely how Jerrell felt—betrayed. Hoodwinked. Like these Hamptons girls might have pulled the wool over their eyes with their sophisticated personalities, clothes, and money.

Jerrell had only been saying aloud what Sheldon had questioned in private—if he and his brother's noses had been so wide open over these girls, and they'd committed too soon.

Jerrell only had it wrong in one area. Kevin Middleton was not the source of their problems. Kevin had simply revealed the truth, and understandably so, after Maddy and Chrissy had burned the man.

The Rouse men needed to deal with their women.

Right after he ordered his coffee and jumped onto his phone for emails, he and another body backed into one another.

"Oh, excuse me," a female voice said next to him.

"Sorry," he replied at the same time.

When Sheldon raised his eyes, he stared at someone he hadn't seen in a while. "Darian."

Her eyes lifted to find his while she dabbed doughnut glaze from her winter white jacket. "Oh, wow, Sheldon!" Her mouth spread into a smile.

"Long time," he commented.

Before he could stop himself, his eyes were already making their way over her figure, and he was instantly reminded of how often she did yoga and Pilates. Petite, curvy and toned, a clear reminder of her commitment to keeping herself in shape.

"A long time indeed. You've kept yourself well. Good to see you." Her smile was easy and warm as always. "How have you been? I heard you were getting married soon. Congratulations."

He remembered their last conversation a year ago, and her distraught pleas when he broke up with her by phone. "Thank you. I'm doing pretty well. And yourself?"

Oh, the days when he was free to date whomever he wanted. No kids, no ex-husband, no attachments. No Kevin Middleton or silly turf wars among rich kids that left him dizzy and overwhelmed some days.

"Good! I got a promotion at work, did some traveling, had a pretty chill year," she said with a grin. "Can't complain at all."

"Darian!" The barista called out her name with her coffee.

"Well, that's me. It was really good to see you, Sheldon. I wish you all the best. You look different somehow." She squinted and her head cocked to the side. "I hope that's a good thing."

Without a whiff of hesitation, melancholy or nostalgia on her, she didn't wait for his response before she turned to walk away.

The last time they spoke, she was begging him to give their relationship a shot. Not this time. She reached out to grab her cup, and Sheldon understood the reason for her contentment. A gorgeous diamond solitaire now blessed her left hand. As she made her exit, a suave guy approached, who reached out to her and threw Sheldon a quick glance, possibly asking her who Sheldon was. Her hand caressed the dude's jaw, before they headed out together. She didn't look back.

For a few seconds, Sheldon recalled Darian's simplicity. There was nothing complicated about her. She held down her job as a stockbroker, and had wanted a husband and kids. The simple life.

Right then, his cell phone vibrated with a text message from Chrissy.

Chrissy: *Judge set a hearing in two weeks about Blake getting the kids on Christmas Day.*

Blake Mason, the guy Sheldon might have hated as much as his brother hated Kevin Middleton.

For the most part, the year had been good for his and Chrissy's family. Little Blake was thriving and had become one of the top little league football players in the state. He was no longer having behavioral issues at school and was a school representative for his class. Mostly A's on his report card and one B in Math that he and Sheldon were working on. And now that Sheldon's own son was living with them, the two boys had become inseparable.

The last thing their household needed was the likes of Blake. Sheldon was already questioning—or rather, dreading—the secrets of Chrissy's minefield marriage to the man. And Sheldon feared the bomb that might go off from Chrissy's dealings with Blake.

"Daddy!" Kara screamed that evening as Shel walked through the door after work.

The house was a mess with toys strewn throughout the open walkway and the boys' schoolbooks scattered around the living room. Sheldon smiled to himself. This current scenario differed greatly from a year before, when his last house sat hollow and lonely.

"Baby girl, you had a good day at school?" he asked, picking up Chrissy's daughter, whom he now considered to be his daughter also.

"Yeah."

"*Yeah?* You mean *yes?*" he asked.

She lowered her head up and down bashfully. "*Yes,* we made pine cone Christmas trees. I made one with your name and one with Mommy's name."

"Oh, really?" Sheldon shook his head at her outfit with paint and glitter all over it. "I can't wait to see how all that looks in your room. Where are your brothers?"

"Outside with the football," she whispered, and Sheldon knew she lowered her voice because she was ashamed to be snitching.

He lowered her before heading through the French doors, standing out on the terrace, hands on his hips. "Gentlemen, is homework finished? And if it is, the chores certainly aren't. You two know the rules. Bring it on in and wash up for dinner."

"What are we having?" Hadar asked.

"A special casserole called 'get washed up and find out,'" Sheldon joked.

"Mr. Rouse, glad to have you home. I tried to tell them,

but you know how sneaky Blake can be," the babysitter said apologetically.

"No worries, Deanne. Thanks for watching them. I got it now."

The only reason he and Chrissy overlooked the babysitter talking on the phone with her boyfriend was she lived up the street and could often come on short notice. For now, anyway, he couldn't fire her for letting the boys run over her.

After they ate the pizza he ordered, they wrapped up homework, did chores, and then sat in the living room so the boys could take turns reading from *The Nutcracker in Harlem*.

All of them kicked back in their socks and pajamas until Chrissy video-conferenced into Alpine from Sag Harbor.

Over the video conference, Shel set the Portal device down on the coffee table, so she could participate in the family chat.

With her tired eyes and lazy smile, she spoke to the children and placed curlers in her hair.

Even at six months pregnant, with her face a little plumper, her body fuller, and the weight of pregnancy bearing on her, Chriselle was the most beautiful angel he'd ever seen.

Her movements were still confident and sexy as hell, even in her tired state. The steely determination still focused her eyes as she questioned each child about what they accomplished at school that day, and what personal fear they worked to overcome. Her mouth was still sensual, and he watched with longing as she sucked one of her lips intently while she listened. He wished those voluptuous breasts were sitting in front of him now to suck. Her full face was wrapped in smooth, candy–coated skin.

"Baby? Are you still with us?" she asked Sheldon.

Now it was Sheldon who smiled bashfully. "Sorry, sweetheart, my fear…" He stared at her directly as she and the children waited. "No, I have not worked on my fear today."

Chriselle studied him from the other side of the screen. Their eyes held one another, and he sensed that she already knew his deepest fear.

"Why didn't you work on your fear, Daddy?" Kara asked.

Sheldon stroked her hair, and continued exchanging his worry with Chrissy. "Because I didn't try. I'm still too scared, baby girl."

His statement was loaded. And he was certain Chrissy detected it.

"Okay, you guys, time for bed. Dad is going to take you up," Chrissy said.

"Love you, Dad," Hadar said, leaning in for a lazy hug before heading off to his room.

"I love you too, young man," Sheldon replied, still feeling the tap-dance of his heart, upon hearing Hadar say it.

"Love you, Dad," Blake said, throwing his arms around Sheldon and peering up at him.

"Love you too, Son," Sheldon said.

"Love you, Daddy," Kara murmured.

"Love you too, baby girl." Sheldon kissed the top of her head.

Blake's arms still lingered around Sheldon. "Dad?"

"Yeah, man, what's up?"

"When my Dad and me talked on the phone the other night, he said we'll be with him for Christmas in California, and there's nothing you or Mom can do about it." In the boy's face, he seemed agonized. "I wanted to be here with you so we can play ball, and I can see Rome." He referenced Roland's son, who was also part of their little clique with Hadar. A clique Sheldon was proud of, just as he was proud of his own brothers. "I want to play with our new toys and eat Grandma Pauletta's food. Are me and Kara going to have to leave?"

"First of all, it's Dad and *I* talked. And Kara and *I*. Second of all, how do you know you're getting some new toys?" Sheldon asked. "You're getting too old for toys. You'll be twelve pretty soon."

Blake's face scrunched up, as he looked at Sheldon with disgust. "But I only just turned eleven!"

"That doesn't matter. Suck it up and take it like a man."

From the Portal device a few feet away, Chrissy's laughter sputtered out.

"But, Dad!" Blake started to beg, while both he and Sheldon chuckled.

"*But Dad* nothing. How do you know your Mom and *I* have money? This new house cost a lot. Your school clothes were a grip. And I already showed you the bill for your football. From where I stand, you've already had your Christmas, and I'd say you and *I* should be good now, right?"

Blake's mouth fell in half-humor, half-horror, his eyes searching Sheldon desperately to see if he was only kidding.

Once Shel saw that he'd taken the boy's mind off the custody issue, Sheldon took Blake's head in both his hands. "Chill out, man. Whatever happens, your mom and I will be right there too. If you go to California, we all go. Wherever you are, we'll do it together. Now, go get in bed. And stop thinking about Christmas presents you're not getting."

Blake spun around as his body shook with chuckles.

His energy full of his family, next, he gazed at the delicious face of the woman carrying his child.

The year had been a blessed one, including her performances, deals, and signing her own talent, and the exposure she'd gotten from it. With the successful opening of *Dream Stage*, she and her friends had saved an integral part of New York's Black history. Bookings for the facility extended well into the next year.

But the year had also come with its challenges. That involved constant custody battles with Blake, paying for expensive security to ensure that no new threats arose, managing the children's school and activities, and sometimes going days without seeing one another when working.

And yet, Sheldon wanted Chris as his wife more than anything.

Seeing Darian today changed nothing. It only reminded him of how boring she was.

Talking to his sweetheart now had his heart firing on all cylinders.

Though he and Chrissy were exhausted, his sense of peace and purpose were sitting on a full tank. What a difference a year with her had made.

"So, when are we putting up a Christmas tree?" she asked.

His laugh was soft, as he turned out the lights and made his way upstairs. "Who said you were getting a Christmas tree? With all that money you're spending on the wedding, I don't have time for you either."

As always, all thirty-two of her teeth showed. "It just so happens I have a personal quid pro quo relationship with Santa."

Humor shook his chest. "Is that right? What can you do for Santa that I can't do?"

Her cheeks lifted as she kept smiling, and her graceful hands opened her silk robe to display her swollen breasts. Pregnancy had only made Chrissy sexier. Meatier.

And she *knew* it.

"You'd be surprised at my gifts that Santa loves. And he doesn't even have to wait for Christmas."

Sheldon's blood might have started boiling. His teeth grabbed his bottom lip, and he gripped his rigid wood. "Alright. I see. So… I think I can head out to the forest, chop down a Christmas tree… or five." A large exhale escaped him. He would wait for the kids to start snoring before he handled his erection himself. "Damn, I wish you were here so I could hold you. Among other things."

"I wish I was there too, so you can calm down your kicking little girl. It seems like you're the only one who can." Chriselle rubbed her belly and her tired face shined at him. "She's a lot like her mama. She only settles down when she hears Daddy's voice."

Staring at her, Sheldon was the happiest man alive. His love and admiration for Chrissy were not a question. She was head and shoulders more woman than Darian. Just thinking about all of Chrissy's grown womanhood got his dick jumping. Even though they had rough, exhausting days, he wouldn't trade it to go back to his previous unfulfilling life.

Concerned Little Blake might overhear, Sheldon avoided mentioning Blake Senior by name. "I don't agree with the request."

"Me neither. But he hasn't made any new threats in months, and he's almost finished with a fifty-two-week DV class."

"Just five months ago, he was calling you to his hotel room, trying to intimidate you. And he was half-way through his DV class then. That dude is just going through the motions. He hasn't changed. He's only biding his time."

Chrissy sighed. "I agree. But there's been no incidents with the kids, and I'm not sure we can stop him this go round."

Sheldon thought about that. One of his friends in data information had been collecting intel on Blake all year. Shel still hadn't told Chrissy, but he knew for a fact that Blake was still tied up in illicit international money deals.

However, this time, Sheldon couldn't run bank traces, the way he had that summer. Doing it too many times might raise suspicions on his job. And he didn't want to rely on hackers too much, as it increased the likelihood of criminal exposure. His mind had already begun navigating how he could get the information he needed.

"I love you, baby," he whispered to her.

"I love you too, Daddy."

A large question still loomed between them, but he

would not ask it right now. Not over the Internet. Regardless of what she may have done, or what she knew—and the worry that wrapped around his chest like barbed wire —he would do anything for her.

Anything.

After they got off the Portal, he picked up his encrypted, secure phone. Taking a breath, he thought for a moment.

After all the hard work he and Chrissy had done to get Little Blake on track, now Blake Senior wanted to waltz back into their lives? Without proving he had the kids' best interests at heart, Blake thought he could unravel everything?

Was Sheldon wrong for believing these were *his* kids now?

He made the call.

"What's up, man?" The voice on the other end answered.

Unsure if he should do this, Sheldon pressed on. "I did you a solid a few days ago. Now I need one from you."

"I'm listening."

"I need to know where Blake Mason keeps his last stash."

Silence bore down on America's only two Black tech moguls.

Sheldon continued, "You get me that, and I'll get my brother on board."

Another pause. The younger man was thinking.

"All right," Kevin Middleton replied. "Done."

ADELLA

*A*della's menstrual cycle was a day late, and now her nervous fingers ripped open a pregnancy test.

As soon as Desmond had left to go help Jerrell, and

before she headed to *Dream Stage* to look over financials and budget needs.

Her family home was empty after all the relatives had left. With jitters, she waited for results and made coffee.

Now that their first six months of marriage had passed, and they'd settled in with each other, she had gotten to know Desmond more. She was now confident their marriage wasn't a fluke. He really was in this with her.

Early on, she'd nursed concerns that he still only wanted money and validation that came with being married to a high-society doctor. The way they had been thrown together by their families, she'd had her doubts. She'd questioned if she could bring children into the kind of loveless marriage her parents had.

But pouring her coffee, she chuckled to herself. Desmond had learned to cook three good meals consistently. He was more than halfway through his business program and had been offered the assistant manager position at the brewery where he worked in Boston. Every day that they looked into each other's eyes, she saw his growing dedication. And it was growing in her.

Now she wanted a large family with him. A year ago, she was questioning whether being with Wes was the right move.

Today, she couldn't see making it through the day without Desmond and his goofy humor.

Nervous legs carried her back to the bathroom. Heart pumping in her throat, she sniffed a big breath, and held it.

Looked down.

Her balloon popped.

Negative.

Her hand flew to cover the sudden shriek of despair. They'd been trying for three months. Shaking overtook her, against her toughest efforts not to break down. But the hopelessness she'd been fighting rocked her chest and vibrated through the rest of her.

She struggled to breathe. But her diaphragm refused to assist.

What was wrong with her? Why was her womb empty when the heart sitting inside her had so much to give? Why was she inadequate?

All the times people doubted Adella, she was able to prove them wrong. She always proved her capability.

Not this time.

Mother Nature was not some human obstacle that Del could overcome, and the reality of that poured from Adella in sob after sob.

A knock at the door startled her.

Immediately, she grabbed the bathroom towel, buried her face in it. She attempted to find the game face that evaded her. Then, she grabbed the testing stick, not wanting to throw it in the trash for cleanup staff to find and know her business. Having no pockets to place it in, she wrapped it in the towel, and dabbed at her eyes one last time.

Another knock scraped the bathroom door. She thought everyone had left. When had someone entered the house?

"Del? You in there?" Solomon asked from the other side of the door.

Her big brother. What was he doing here? He rarely came around anymore, except for when the other family was here to visit. Since he had opened up his new restaurant *Taste*, running it had pretty much taken over his life. He had abandoned her, and their grandfather's company, leaving her to figure it out on her own.

She pulled the door open between them. "Solly, what's up?"

"Did I just hear you in here crying?"

His face seemed to carry genuine concern. It shocked her. The few times she'd seen him this year, his eyes had felt like a fiery anvil.

"I didn't know anybody else was here. You don't usually come by when I'm here,." Del made sure to shake some hot sauce on her tone as she said it.

He rolled his tongue over his teeth. "I wanted to talk about this Business Council thing Pastor Arnold wants us all to do. Thought I'd stop by and see if you had left yet." He leaned inside the door frame, placing his hands on either side of it, staring at her. For a smidgeon of a moment, it almost felt like old times. She very much wanted to go into her big brother's arms, so he could put a Band-Aid over her broken heart.

"So, why are you in here sobbing?"

Del shook her head. "It's nothing. What about the Council did you want to talk about?"

His gaze deepened, and he examined her. "I know we don't talk much anymore, and Papa's passing through us for a loop…"

"Threw us for a loop, Solomon?" Del snapped, forgetting her negative test for a moment. Now she practically collapsed under the weight of all the changes and challenges she had endured this year. "That's the understate-ment of the year. You *sued* me!"

"I've been running that company for years, Del! You could have walked away from the inheritance and turned it down, out of respect!"

"But apparently, that's not the way Papa wanted it. Or he would not have left it to me. Besides, even if I *had* turned down the inheritance and walked away, you *still* would not have gotten the company. An administrator would've run the company for years, until the next generation came up. *Then*, if nobody was interested, it would've been split among everybody, into pieces. If anything, I prevented that from happening. You didn't have to storm off like a child who lost his toy! I invited you to stay and help run it."

Solomon rocked on his heels as if he hated being reminded. "Let's drop it. This is not getting us anywhere."

"Fine. So, what is it then?" she asked, running her hand around the back of her neck, flustered that she couldn't sit down with her one sibling and have a simple conversation.

"*Dream Stage* needs to join the Council. Since you all were awarded *Soul of the Sag*, and we are clearly going to be sharing parking with you all, we should probably coordi-nate schedules for next year. It makes the most sense if *all* the businesses signed on so we can start having meetings, create a shared email exchange, and discuss logistics, promo runs and campaigns next year. We can make sure we're not clashing with one another."

"I can't believe you're working with Kevin Middleton," she huffed, not hiding her disdain.

Solomon's face actually softened now. "Me either. It

was Keenan's idea to bring him in. But I can't say his being around has been a bad thing."

"Oh yeah, by the way, congratulations on Sasha Static," Del muttered, sipping her coffee.

"That was all Middleton. I must say, the man is not short on big ideas." He poured himself a cup.

The creamer sat next to her hand. Recalling how he liked lots of cream, she held it toward him. Solly raised his cup, and she poured.

The small gesture was a major moment, since it was the *only* bonding they'd done this year.

"Kevin's my enemy. He tormented me, Solomon." She leaned against the counter, most likely to bolster herself while she bench-lifted her next words. "I can't help but wonder, did you hook up with Kevin in business to drive the stake through me? Getting back at me because of Papa's will? You got revenge against me by running to *Kevin*, of all the people?"

Solly faced her straight on. "No. I asked Keenan not to invite Kevin. But Keenan has his own mind, and at the end of the day, he gets the last say on Explore. He went and offered a partnership to Kevin anyway." Her tall brother of six feet and three inches raised his long arms in the air. "Even though I hate the guy, Kevin's addition to our partnership has been nothing but gold. He's a damn good businessman."

Adella rolled her eyes. "Tell me about it. He whipped us good this fall."

Solomon nodded in agreement. "He did. Maddy and Chrissy took it too far with that whole Harvard leak. I don't like the guy, but not even I would have taken it that far."

Her brother then studied her once again, and she could always tell when another truth was coming.

"As far as you and I are concerned," Solly continued, "do I want to see your little ass pay for taking what was rightfully mine, and not turning it over to me? Yes. But would I intentionally hurt you with Kevin Middleton? No. And I swear that on Papa's grave."

His gaze fell soft for a moment.

Del nodded, satisfied.

Somewhat.

"If Maddy and Chrissy join the Council, I'm in. But Maddy's not coming without Jerrell. And Jerrell's not coming unless Kevin drops dead. Can't say I blame J."

"I know. We're working on that. Can you just focus on Maddy though?" he asked. Before she had a chance to answer, Solomon's eyes switched subjects before his mouth did. "I want you to know that I *will* try taking the company back, Del."

She nodded again. "I know. You want to see me fail."

Still holding the coffee cup, he aimed an index finger. "No. Not fail. Just recognize that real estate is not your wheelhouse."

"You weren't doing a very good job running it, so it wasn't yours either," Del shot back.

Solly's jaw clenched again, and they were right back to square one.

He set down his mug, a sign the conversation was over. It deflated her.

With one step of his long legs, he leaned over her and

planted a kiss on her forehead. "See you at Chrissy's wedding."

Once he reached the door, he stopped, as if hit by a final thought.

"And don't worry, Del. You're a good person. Your babies will come."

Adella gasped as he walked out.

Though they had spoken little all year, he had known. Solly always had been an old soul who saw more than most.

ME TOO

JERRELL

reaking wood emphasized the stiff silence between Maddy and Jerrell that Sunday night, during Jerrell's turn to travel to D.C. Her socked feet barely touched the floor as they hung from her great-grandmother's restored wooden, rocking chair. In her arms, a contented Chase's eyes grew heavy while sucking on her breast.

The nights when Jerrell was back in New York, he would watch the two of them over FaceTime. Even if he was appearing at an event, or working late at one of his stores, he never missed a night of Chase and Maddy. Of watching his seed close his eyes and fly to heaven on his mother's breast. Encircled by Maddy's wings.

Until two months ago, the preciousness of this sight punctuated his day. Made his heart swell with admiration. As if seeing an angel give life to his child. To their family.

Now… courtesy of Kevin Fucking Middleton… Jerrell was haunted by the nightmare of his angel on a school desk, fucking some old guy…

"I should probably take a look at that, make sure it doesn't break." He finally spoke in this moment, using the whining wood as an excuse to break the monotony.

Without a word or a glance, Chase still in her arms, she got up. And walked to the bedroom. He ignored her attitude and got a flat screwdriver out of the kitchen drawer. He started to jerk the arms and other areas of the chair to find the source of the squeaking.

"Be careful with it. It's an antique."

He looked up. She was glaring from the bedroom.

"Glad you've got a mouth to finally say *something* this weekend. You act like *I'm* the one who fucked my way up the ladder." He couldn't help himself.

Silent wrath was her response.

Jerrell knew she was only quelling her anger for Chase. But from the glare in her eye, Maddy would pay him back later. Since he had arrived in D.C., Friday afternoon, she had distanced herself. She'd kept all their exchanges formal, all business, limiting her conversation to Chase and his needs.

Dutifully, Jerrell checked the legs and rungs on the chair. As he did, he recalled when he and her brother William had moved the rocking chair into her brownstone over summer. They had put together Chase's crib, diaper dispenser, and other baby items, preparing her brownstone for Chase's arrival. Even though she had spent much of her early pregnancy in D.C., Jerrell had struggled with knowing they'd be apart. But he'd swallowed it. Maddy Cakes meant the world to him. She'd worked so hard to get where she was, and he was determined to support her ambitions.

He now wondered what corrupt ambition he had sacrificing for. For what corrupt individual.

"When do you want to go and get Chase's Santa pictures taken? Do you want to do it here, or in Sag Harbor?" The mere question tasted like Santa's foot in his mouth, at the thought they might not be taken in New York.

"Doesn't matter to me. You decide," she answered.

The Eastern frost may as well have been sitting in her throat.

"Fine. We can do it back in the Sag when you guys come up this weekend."

"Fine."

"Christmas tree?" he asked.

"We can put one up at your place, since we'll be there for Chris and Shel anyway," she muttered.

"Fine," he huffed.

"Fine."

Once the baby stopped sucking, he wasn't quite asleep yet, and she pulled him from her nipple. The handoffs to Jerrell were the only times they'd touched that weekend.

Even though she pissed him off, he fought the searing urge to lean down and kiss Maddy. Normally, she would tilt her head up and they'd kiss. Now, she hauled off to do some evening reading through her Capitol Hill files. Always grinding. Never ceasing.

As proud of her as Jerrell was, was he wrong for hating her job? For secretly wishing she would give it up and come to New York, and be with him, sleep next to him, wake up next to him?

His hot and cold emotions whipped up a storm inside him. He wished he could incinerate Kevin Middleton.

Kevin may as well have set Jerrell's house on fire. Now Maddy's husband was left to sort through the ashes of distrust left behind.

What would Maddy really be—*where* would she be—if she had not done it? What Middleton said she had done.

Of all the people who could've revealed this, Jerrell had to hear it from the man he hated most. Jerrell did not want to think that dude's name, let alone utter it.

Finally, once Chase fell asleep, he couldn't take it anymore. When he put his son down, he asked his wife, "How did you feel? When you saw him with Cher?"

Maddy rolled her eyes, obviously sick of this line of questioning, or not wanting to be reminded of the feelings she might've still carried. "I didn't feel. Okay? I felt nothing. Except sympathy for Cher. A little bit of worry that she might get hurt. That he will say or do something to her that'll crush her. Other than that, Jerrell, no, I felt nothing. I know that's hard for you to accept, but it's true."

"How did he know about you and—"

"Kevin has lowdown ways of obtaining information. Contacts in the technology hacker world, just as many connections as I do, probably more."

Squeezing his head, Jerrell wished he could stop. Wished he could turn off the myriad questions on his brain. But he had committed to living with this woman for the rest of his *life*.

"Why did you and Chrissy leak the shit about that dude's school?" Jerrell refused to say his name. "Why couldn't you just let it be? Why do you always need to keep up beef with him?"

Maddy stalled with an answer, as did her eyes that darted everywhere.

"To remind him he's not as invincible as he thinks he is."

Jerrell stepped closer to her, until only inches separated them. "Why do you *care*... what he thinks?"

Mrs. Rouse's eyes flickered a moment before hardening. "If you were going to torture me about him, I seriously wish you would never have married me."

With his chest sagging into his feet, weighing them down, Jerrell pivoted out of the room, to sleep on the couch. "Me too."

JERRELL FLED from the bite of New York cold. He thrust himself inside the doorway of *Ashford & Simpson's Sugar Bar.* Halfway through the day, his clothes were still halfway arranged. His khakis and knitted sweater clung for dear life to a body exhausted after he'd drunk himself into another sleepless night.

Tugging at his heart was a longing to see and hold his kid. And yes, even his hard-headed wife. Prickly whiskers of his five o'clock shadow scraped his hand that attempted to wipe fatigue from his face.

Where was Xavier? His former co-worker had asked him out to lunch. Jerrell wasn't sure if he wanted to catch up or rub Jerrell's face in his new promotion.

Now that he was no longer a free-wheeling stunner on Wall Street, the new dad hoped he didn't look too much like a startup businessman struggling to stay afloat.

Low, yellow restaurant lighting made it hard to see past all the bodies, to find a particular face.

Jerrell checked his watch. 3:30 p.m. He had arrived on time.

The dim lights brightened, and he blinked a few times to adjust his eyesight.

"Jerrell!"

Clapping began at a low hum and soon roared.

Confused, he stared around him. Everybody in the restaurant was one of his old co-workers. His body rocked from the hands slapping his back.

"Congratulations, Man! It's been a year, and you haven't come back begging for a job!" Xavier Douglas teased him.

His former Wall Street colleagues laughed.

Damn. It was a surprise party. Jerrell had been so busy the past year, between meeting and marrying Maddy, traveling to Washington, D.C., to ensure he was present for his son, and managing three *Poppin Pauletta's* locations, the catering events, and preparing to expand beyond New York next year.

He had completely forgotten that, a year ago, he had left his secure banking job, high-paying salary, cushy office and benefits, and cut out on his own. And then met Maddy.

"So, tell us! What's life like on the other side?" one of his colleagues yelled out.

"Yeah, tell us how good it feels to taste freedom!" Someone else called to him.

"Go on. Brag about what it's like not to have a boss to report to every day. You're your own freaking boss!"

They all started applauding again.

Jerrell scratched his head. "Ha. Let's see. I feel about as free as a debtor sitting in jail, hoping I make enough sales to pay rent from month to month," Jerrell reported. The room hummed with chuckles. "But in all honesty, though it's daunting and sometimes I feel like Bug's Bunny being shot at by Elmer Fudd, I would not trade running my own show for anything in the world, other than my son." He stopped and thought for a moment. "And my wife."

"Wow! Why is Maddy an afterthought now? You running for the exits already, Rouse?"

He knew he had to clean it up quickly. "Of course not. It's just, as most of you already know, there is nothing on

Earth like looking at your child who came from you. Other than that experience, I get to wake up every day and decide my destiny. That is breathtaking, but also breath-snatching." Jerrell laughed, and the room laughed with him.

"And not only are you a boss now, you're also married to a hot wife, who might be going to the White House!" Xavier called.

"What should we start calling you? Mr. First Man? Your Highness? His Majesty? Do you think Maddy could become the first Black female President?"

One of the women exhaled and shook her head in amazement, expressing awe at Jerrell's wife. "Boy, I tell you, the brains on that woman. I heard her on a CNN interview a few weeks back. The way she was answering all those questions, without batting an eye… like she eats information for breakfast. And I read in a magazine article how she impressed the President even when she was in college. You must be so proud."

Jerrell unfurled his tongue from the top of his mouth.

"I really appreciate you guys for this."

He couldn't get out any more words. When he started his grandmother's business a year ago, gave two-weeks' notice, and then stormed out of his father's Wall Street office, he had no clue what he would do next. Where his high stakes roll of the dice would land. Back then, every day for months, in the NASCAR racetrack of his bloodstream, his anxiety had sped like the rush of sports cars.

Now, remembering how he'd survived it, he started to choke up. Jerrell's shoulders shook. The bar broke into applause and cheering.

He had no idea any of his old co-workers had been

paying attention. Sure, they were now using his business to cater most of the bank's events. But he now sent his community relations reps and catering team to handle much of it. Jumping from bed in the wee hours of the morning, running from one location to another daily, he often felt alone. And was not aware that his old running buddies had cared.

Or of how far he had come.

THE TRUTH

SHELDON & CHRISSY

SHELDON

Sheldon stopped in front of the Salvation Army red drop-in bucket, where a worker in a Santa hat was ringing the bell. He pulled out the wads from his pocket and dropped it in the slot, before the worker's weathered face managed a tired but grateful smile.

Within a few more paces, he was standing at the entrance to Jerrell's pastry shop in the city. He could barely get in. Bodies crowded the front door as customers pressed against one another, pushing to escape the frigid cold and feel at least a little heat from inside the store.

"Excuse me," Sheldon said while he tried squeezing through. Though he hadn't entered the door yet, smells of his Gram's kitchen entered his nose immediately. Pastries both sweet and savory took him back decades, to his Louisiana childhood.

"The end of the line is back there, Mister," someone muttered.

Sheldon laughed at that. Especially as he recalled how empty this place was just one year ago, when Jerrell first opened.

"I work here," he lied with a chuckle.

His tailored Theory wool coat, Dior pinstripe suit and Salvatore Ferragamo oxfords clearly indicated he did not. But in a sense, he had provided some of the initial seed money for his little brother to start out, and Shel had helped make this *Pauletta's* concept a reality. There was no way he would stand in line.

Finally managing to stuff himself through the front

door, he headed toward the counter. There, a rather youngish girl was ringing up customers. He couldn't help noticing she wore a fitted sweater, with the neckline cut low enough that there was no neckline; but more of a breast-line, displaying her healthy rack that must've been a double *some*thing. Sheldon briefly wondered who she thought she'd be feeding all that meat to.

Jerrell's assistant manager noticed Sheldon and quickly waved while running around, bagging orders and making coffee. Throwing a head nod, Shel made his way to the back kitchen. *Good God*, as soon as he opened the door, feverish activity and tasty aromas called him back home to New Orleans.

Pecans, walnuts, sweet potatoes, brown sugar, nutmeg, cinnamon, peaches, bananas, blueberries, powdered cocoa, piping hot fudge, vanilla extract, cream cheese, rum, whisky and Grand Marnier dominated the cabinet tops.

At the large, stainless-steel ovens, his great Aunt Rose and his grandma, for whom the business was named, *Poppin' Pauletta*, whipped, poured, and beat ingredients into Christmas magic.

He went to tower over the tiny woman who once whipped him with a switch at the bus stop. For gambling and hustling kids out of their lunch money. It was his and Roland's first joint venture.

"Hey, Gram," he said, leaning in to kiss her jaw.

She jumped. "Oh, my Lord! Boy, quit scaring your grandmama like that. Where did you come from? I didn't think I was gon' see you again 'til next year. You boys done got all wrapped up with them high-saditty girls," she said, patting him back before moving on to her next set of pastries.

"I need to holler at you for a minute, Gram. It won't take long. I know you're famous now and everything, but it'll just be a minute. It's important," Sheldon said.

But he didn't have to beg. Before he finished, she was already wiping off her hands and waving him toward the office.

"Well, come on, Grandson, out with it. I don't make as much money as you, but I'm twice as busy." She swallowed some drops of water with her diabetes medication.

"You're worth far more than I'll ever be, baby girl," he replied. "It's J, Gram."

"Okay?" She lifted an eyebrow. "Ain't it always?"

He shrugged. "Alright, good point. But it's different now. His stubbornness could put this business in jeopardy. The Black residents in the Hamptons, the Black elders and leadership—especially Pastor Arnold—all want the Black business-owners to form a council together. To coordinate with each other's schedules, support one another's events, and iron out conflicts. They don't want anymore of this competition stuff. They're working to create more unity. But J's not with it."

"Well, why does he feel like that? Jerrell can be hot-headed, but he doesn't just get mad without a reason, so what else is going on?"

"Kevin Middleton. There was a situation a few weeks ago, when Kevin came to the house and disclosed a secret about Madison that J didn't know."

That statement knitted his grandmother's eyebrows together. "Well? What was it?"

Sheldon winced. "Out of respect, I'd rather not say. But it happened years ago, when Maddy was still in school. And J can't let it go. It's been messing with him. Bad."

She thought a moment. "Hmph. So that's the reason he's been coming in here some mornings smelling like Bacchus Sunday."

The joke shook her grandson's shoulders. "Anyway, Kevin is also joining this Council because he's one of the co-owners for Explore, which owns Taste in the Hamptons. J has always beefed with Kevin over Maddy. But now, with this new information Kevin had, J refuses to play ball. He wants no part of any setup involving Kevin."

Pauletta's eyebrow cocked. "Can't say I blame that boy. Who wants to walk around with another man that knows as much as you do about your wife's snatch?"

Sheldon huffed. "Gram, I get it. I do. But Jerrell needs to man up. I deal with people in my industry who would knife me in my sleep if they could. I still have to go in there, smile, and treat them like we're best friends. J's a business-owner now. His emotional decision-making doesn't just affect him anymore. They affect his employees and his bottom line. Like it or not, Kevin carries weight in the Hamptons. It is what it is. J can't keep walking around pouting forever. If he doesn't do this—"

"Alright. Alright, okay." She held up her hands in surrender. "I'll talk to him. When are y'all taking me to dinner?" she asked with a wink, already heading out.

"Oh, so you're charging me for this?" Sheldon joked.

"Damn straight. Besides, when y'all want to eat is the only time I get to see ya now. It's high time *you* provided food. This weekend?"

"Maddy will be here from D.C. this weekend. You should probably address J before she arrives. So you can help him get his head right," Sheldon said, scheming as always. "Tomorrow night? I'll tell J to come meet up here. And I'll also invite Roland, Kamila and Etta, so it won't look like—"

"So it won't look like you're scheming on your brother, like you always do?" she said, pursing her lips and stretching her arms out for a hug.

A chuckling Sheldon went into them. "Yes, ma'am."

Her thin arms could have been unbreakable vines as they circled him tight. "Dare I say it, Boy, but with all that scheming you do, you just might be the glue that holds this family together when I'm gone."

"Don't talk like that, Gram. You'll live forever."

"Tell that to this old heart of mine, barely ticking."

He kissed her forehead before they parted. "It's carrying all that love you give."

A FEW MINUTES LATER, after lunch, Sheldon was back in his office.

"Sheldon?" his secretary buzzed him.

"Yeah, Estaire?"

"There's someone here requesting to see you. He's downstairs, being held by security at the front of the building. His name is Blake Mason."

Sheldon wasn't surprised. As soon as Kevin had gotten

him the information, he'd had Chrissy's attorney send it to Blake's counsel, as an implicit threat. Of what could unfold at the custody hearing if Blake moved forward.

"That's fine. After they search him, let him come up." Sheldon took out his encrypted phone, pressed the 'record' feature, and placed it at the edge of his desk.

What could he say?

His grandmother was right.

He was always thinking. Always.

Then, he took out his regular phone and shot a text to his security agent, who was lying low in a vehicle on the street. *I'm going into a meeting with Blake Mason. Come on up.*

As much as Sheldon would have loved to throw down, just like in the backwoods of Louisiana, get in a few blows and release some tension, his and Chrissy's new mansion had a mortgage on it, and they had a baby on the way.

Standing up, he sat against his desk and was waiting when Estaire escorted Blake in.

"Mason," Sheldon said, not moving to extend his hand.

"Mr. Rouse, I won't waste your time. As you probably guessed, I'm here to discuss the issue of my children. *My* children." He spoke through clenched teeth.

Sheldon brushed off nothing from his pant legs. "*Our* children. What about them?"

"In case you haven't checked their birth certificates—"

"And I don't need to. In case *you* haven't checked their school records, test scores, behavioral assessments, after-school activities, teacher write-ups and their mental well-being over the last six months, they're doing just fine without you. So, if you want to come in here and tell me you have a right to unsupervised visits off the simple fact that your blood runs through them, miss me with the bullshit." Sheldon folded his arms, fully prepared for round two. "Now, what's your next order of business?"

An irritated Blake throws his weight into his next points. "Was my lawyer correct that you also had your son taken from you? That you were without your boy for three years? Your wife left you, without a word? Just like mine hauled out of California without telling me? So how can you turn around and do to another man the same that's been done to you, man?"

Sheldon was unmoved. "Apples and oranges, dude. Our situations are nowhere near the same. I never lifted a finger against Genie. I've never withheld money or support from her, or made moves to intimidate her, out of spite, not even when I thought she was wrong. And *no* judge has ever needed to protect my son from me, since I've never engaged in criminal behavior, Blake. So don't try and compare yourself to me, because *you're* not *me*."

Blake's body stiffened and shook as if seizing. "I want to visit my kids without a monitor. Is that too much to ask? Chrissy will continue to keep custody. For *now*."

"The problem is we don't trust you with no monitor. Just four months ago, you called Chrissy to your hotel, even though she had a restraining order on you. You were ready to violate it. So you could do God knows what to her? You haven't changed. But your children have. They're happy. They're not listening to a man berate their mother. Blake's not jumping in his sleep anymore. He's not scared he'll get yelled at when he plays a sport, and he's not starting fights to impress you."

Sheldon paused and scratched his neck.

"You are correct though, that I am a father myself, and I would never deny another man access to his kids. I'll talk to Chrissy about you seeing the kids a few hours on Christmas Day. But it'll be here in New York. No unsupervised visits until you've attended a therapist with Blake. And can articulate his needs. Not your needs, but *his*," Sheldon insisted. "Your kids are not puppets for you to manipulate. And if you go to court and try anything else, the judge *will* know what I know… about your *ongoing* activity."

Sheldon sat back again and waited.

Blake's jaw moved around, and then his gaze scraped the carpet fibers. He spent at least a full minute walking in a circle, likely weighing his options. Before he managed to push out, "Fine."

THAT NIGHT, when Sheldon got home, the house buzzed with activity.

Standing in the middle of their open-spaced foyer, between the marble, curving double stairways leading up to the balcony, was a massive Christmas tree.

"Daddy, come help me!" Kara screamed, her joy hugging Sheldon's heart valve.

A hummingbird could have beat its wings inside him. For a moment, watching Kara's face light up, he wondered if he'd made the right call, placing stipulations on Blake the way he had.

He'd made himself a gatekeeper between another man and his family. He tried to imagine how he'd feel if Genie allowed a stranger to do that to him. In fact, Genie *had* allowed a couple of her boyfriends to bogart Hadar.

Then, Little Blake appeared from behind the tree, wearing a grin wider than the white stitching on his football. "Dad? Guess what happened to me today at school?"

"What?" Sheldon asked him.

"A girl asked me for my phone number," the kid replied, beaming.

Sheldon's eyelids tripped, before Chrissy popped from behind the tree. She rubbed her belly, and her lips curled in. She was trying not to crack up.

"What did your mom say?"

"She said talk to you." Little Blake swayed with puppy love.

"I'm hoping you told this chick that you won't be able to talk on the phone, because you'll be homeless."

"Homeless?" Blake repeated.

"Yeah," Sheldon responded, before remembering his parent hat. "*Yes.* Homeless. You will be needing a place to live soon if you think you're going to be talking on the phone before you turn forty."

Hadar laughed, while placing an ornament on the tree. "I told you he wasn't going to let you talk."

"Dude, shut up," Blake said, jerking around.

"Be nice," Sheldon chastised.

"Blake, apologize," Chrissy insisted.

"Sorry," Blake muttered.

Chrissy and Sheldon held a quick eye-conversation, and she tilted her head for him to show some lenience.

Shel capitulated. "If your report card looks good, and you've pulled up on your math like we've been working on, *maybe*, you can talk over the winter break… for two minutes and two seconds… exactly. You will literally say hi and get off the phone. That's it. Whether you get more time depends on your grades staying up."

The sun resurfaced on the boy's face, and sprayed sun flares in every dark spot of Sheldon's chest cavity.

At dinner, they ate Chrissy's pot roast and mashed potatoes with carrots, sitting at the small family table in the kitchen. Occasionally, he gazed up at his fiancée. When not laughing at the kids or cutting Kara's meat or correcting somebody's grammar, they held their own private conversation across the low candlelight burning in the middle.

Despite the question gnawing away at the pit of him, Sheldon wanted more than anything to put the children to bed so he could feel Chrissy's wetness all over his shaft.

After hours of homework, chores, gratitude circle, reading, prayers and putting the kids to bed, they waited to hear snoring.

Sheldon closed the door and moved to Chrissy on the edge of the bed. Gorgeous and radiant as the first night he'd brought her into his home, his love awaited him. They both trembled when he laid his open mouth on hers. Slid his tongue between her soft, satiny lips. A tiny whine floated from his throat when her tongue circled his. As natural as snow falling to the earth, Sheldon's hands descended her shoulders, sweeping off her silk lavender robe. A fleshy piece of heaven awaited him when he bit the nape of her neck.

"Haah." Her breaths were short, excited, tripping over one another.

He slid the spaghetti straps of her silk gown from her shoulders, pulled the bodice over her breasts. Then he gathered her from the bed, swept her into his arms and carried her to the bathroom. Started the shower. Where their mouths rediscovered each other, teeth nibbling. Their fingers shimmied their way down, until they were naked. Sheldon sat on a chair, stuck out his tongue and sucked one swollen tit, absorbing as much as his mouth could handle.

"Mmm," she moaned. Before his fingers entered her canal. He shuddered when he felt the way she dripped for him.

They both rocked through the ecstasy.

While she gyrated on his fingers. He leaned his head against his unborn daughter between them. That Chrissy carried his seed fed his neurosis.

Hot cream slid down his fingers and onto his hand, bringing him over with her. Coming on the seat, his mouth hanging, he exploded with his love.

CHRISSY

Something was on her man's mind.

It had been for weeks. Ever since Kevin's meeting with Maddy. Their enemy had revealed information about both of them. And Chrissy supposed it was only fair, after what she and Maddy had done to Kevin. But still.

Kevin's revelation had been an earthquake sending a fissure down Maddy's and Chrissy's relationships with their men.

This was the same reason Jerrell was now so upset. Sheldon was older, calmer, and had handled it better.

She knew what troubled her soon-to-be-husband.

They entered the shower. He brought the chair inside that he'd bought her, and she rolled her eyes.

"Shel, I'm fine."

It didn't matter. His stare alone compelled her to take the safety seat. He had insisted on her using it because of Genie claiming she fell from a chair in pregnancy during their marriage. Even though it turned out that wasn't really what happened, Sheldon still used an abundance of caution.

He lathered Chrissy with soap, rubbing, cleaning and massaging her back, breasts and belly.

Occasionally, their gazes intersected, and he subliminally asked what she knew he'd been wanting to know. Ever since Jerrell informed Sheldon of what Kevin had told Maddy and Jerrell.

But dutifully, here Sheldon stood, bathing her and protecting her and her children.

Blake's lawyer had contacted hers earlier that day to

report that Blake was standing down. There was no doubt in her mind that this was a result of some play Sheldon had made.

She gripped her man's wrist, stopping him.

She owed him the truth. Even if it meant he would cancel the wedding and their pending marriage.

Shel's eyes wandered to hers.

"Go ahead. Ask me." Her lips quaked while she murmured it.

"Did you do it?"

Chrissy felt the earthquake cracking from him to her. But without blinking, keeping her eyeball focused on his.

Chriselle answered, "Yes."

Sheldon sputtered. A cataclysmic event rocked his chest.

Hurting him, watching him break down, even for a moment, opened a massive rupture inside Chrissy.

She was an accessory to Blake's crimes.

"I asked Lyrical not to go to the police. I told her I would handle him. I didn't know what Little Blake would do seeing his f-father taken away. Or how we would pay for all our properties if he was in jail. I would never ask my parents to shoulder that."

Mashing his fingers into his eyes, Shel seemed to be searching for his resolve. He brought himself to face her again. "Is sh…is she the only one? Are there a-any others?"

Chrissy shook her head. Weak now, and ashamed, she lost sweat from more than sitting in hot water.

Shel's gaze spun down the drain with the pools of water.

His pain reverberated through Chrissy. She wanted

only to go back and relive her entire life, just to be pure and unblemished for Sheldon Rouse.

But Sheldon must've lifted his entire existence, until his eyes met hers again. And he brought her forehead to his. The fierceness in his kiss titillated and terrified her. A firm hand gripped the back of her head. Chrissy squeezed his shoulders, trying not to dig in her nails, but needing him to know how her soul now dragged the floor with shame.

"I'm so sorry, baby."

The shower water fell over their heads.

"What's done is done."

He rose up from his knee, and when he did, she clung to his naked, muscular thighs. Water streamed down his hamstrings, defining their tight curves, his muscular power. The lithe, graceful strength of his body sang of Sheldon's muscle, on several levels.

When Chrissy stared up at him, he held her face, as if reassuring her. But his sadness fell onto her with the water. She ached to comfort him. To apologize with her whole heart. And also to thank him, for whatever he'd done earlier that moved Blake to stand down. But Chrissy wouldn't say it all with words.

She took his dick in her hands. Laid her face against it. Opened her mouth and sucked in the tip. Slowly curled her tongue under his head, the way he liked. In her hands, he shuddered. His length extended. Hardened. Life throbbed in the veins circuiting his manhood. Long, tortured breaths tumbled out of his chest. She pressed his hips to her, until he pumped over and over, and the first part of her man was in her throat. Now, she had learned not to think about her gag reflex, so he could move easier.

But Sheldon surprised her this time, stopping himself. His eyes opened, and descended to her, as did his hand.

A stunned Chrissy stared at him. "Baby, what did you—"

"Together," he said, with resolve. "We strive together. We fuck together."

He helped her from the chair and turned her back to him. He placed her hands against the wall. After kicking the chair in position, he set one of her feet on top of it. Chrissy bucked when Shel's long erection penetrated her. Though they'd been together nearly a year and she now carried his baby, his size *still* stunned her.

Hard and hot, he pumped gently. Her mouth slid down, as she fell into kingdom come. Now with her being pregnant, having the increased blood flow in her canal and heightened nerves, Sheldon's strokes lit up her walls. Her labored breathing skidded along her windpipe.

They intertwined their hands against the shower wall, while lacing their other hands around her belly. Shel thrust faster.

"Your pussy feels even better with my seed inside you." His breaths heated her ear while he clutched her leg.

That her leg was cocked, giving him more leverage, and stroking her sensitive cervix, Chrissy landed on the moon. Throwing her head back against his chest, riding his dick that whipped her over and over, she gave into the wet, gushing climax. When he rolled his hips and kept stroking, Shel dragged out her orgasm. He hooked his length deeper into her.

"Grrrr," she rumbled through the sensational torture.

Shel always rode her like he was claiming her all over

again. Like he always needed to reestablish who she belonged to. He grunted, trembling against her. Linking their hands, they barely stood under the shower water that had turned cold.

Leaning against her temple, Shel kissed her and murmured, "I'll take care of it."

A MOMENT TO BREATHE

ADELLA & DESMOND

ADELLA

*B*ack in Boston after *Dream's* big opening, Adella pushed through the door of the doctors' lockers. Ran her hands over her fatigued body. Squeezed the tension in her neck.

Though the surgery itself had gone well, her patient's other intervening medical conditions still placed her at risk of regressing, and Del worried she still might not make it.

Right now, the heart surgeon's eyes dropped, to perform a visual surgery of her own body. And stopped at her empty womb.

For the past ten years, the practice of medicine had been Del's child. She'd given her care and devotion to her patients, and their well-being. Most of her hard work had been to prove her grandfather right—that she was capable as he said she was. But she often took her patients' struggles onto her shoulders.

Becoming the best doctor often meant caring the most. Staying longer. Arriving earlier. Sharing her patients' fear and hustling to avoid the worst.

Now Del wondered if the bodily strain of saving lives hindered her own body from creating life.

She removed her surgical scrubs and released her kinky Afro from its band. Taking a moment to breathe, her tired head fell into her hands.

"Del," a familiar voice called behind her.

Shocked, Adella turned to see one of the last faces she thought she would ever cross again.

"Wes."

Hands in his pockets, her old boyfriend stepped forward. "I've read about what a phenomenal year you've had."

Stumped as to what to say, she turned on the bench. "Yes, it's been a pretty busy year."

He smiled. "To say the least, huh?"

Del laughed. She'd started a showcase, become famous, had an upcoming book, was now the CEO of her grandfather's real estate company, had fallen out with her family over it, was appearing as a medical expert on news broadcasts, and had been pressed into marriage and *then* fallen in love. "'Pretty busy' is definitely an understatement." She inhaled. "You're here. I thought you hated me."

Just over a year ago, her grandfather's death had upset her entire plan to ultimately marry Wes and move to the countryside.

Wes shook his head. "I could never hate you. You are literally the best of humankind." The snow cascading onto the Boston streets fell in his eyes, for a drop of a moment. "Even though you broke my heart."

Del's hand flew to her mouth. "I came to find you."

"*After* you married him."

"My lawyers advised me against talking before then, because we were gearing up for a lawsuit from my fam—"

He held up his hand. "Doesn't matter now, Del. Not why I came here."

She waited, and braced herself.

"I want to tell you how proud of you I am. All the great things that have happened for you this year, I don't think you would have done all that with me. So maybe your grandfather passing was like the universe pushing you out of your shell, out of your family's shadow, and into greatness. It's been amazing to watch you from afar, how all your stars have lit up. And I mean that."

Adella sniffed back a tiny tear. Not because she missed him. She loved Desmond with her whole heart. But Wes's words resurrected so much that had happened over the past year since her grandfather's death. His passing brought many blessings, but also growing pains and family strife. Emotion overtook her to recount it all.

Starting from the day she'd sent Wes away.

Sometimes she missed Wes's friendship and conversation. They would regularly run patient cases by each other and swap insights and ideas.

"Thank you." She remembered very quickly what she'd read about him. "And congrats on your promotion to head of Pediatric Surgery over at Healing Hands."

"Thanks." He nodded, offering a humble grin. "Adella, I'm proposing to Renee over Christmas. I came to tell you personally, so you wouldn't find out from anybody other than me."

Del had no reaction to that. She was in love with her man and had moved on.

But she and Wes still had unfinished business. "You mean you didn't want me to find out about your marriage the way you found out about mine."

Once again, the winter in his eyes bit her, before he cut them away. "You weren't in love with me. I was the fool."

He was right.

She needed his love until her true love came along.

"I'm sorry, Wes. Not about my marriage or my husband. But the way it ended between us."

Yet again, he shook his head. "It all worked out as it should have. You became who you should have. Had you moved to the country with me, you wouldn't have been happy. It wasn't the city or work you were fleeing; it was the cage others had placed you in. Now you're out of that cage, and you have no need to run." He stuck out his hand toward her. "I hope one day, we'll be friends again. And that we can watch each others' kids grow up."

Taking his hand, she allowed him to lift her from the bench. And they embraced.

"I would like that. Tell Renee she's damn lucky."

"I'm the one," he whispered into her neck, before kissing Del's cheek.

Her grandfather's death had indeed changed things for the best. Had that not happened, she wouldn't have had this phenomenal year. A year in which she had come into her own.

Culminating with the decision she was now about to make.

DESMOND

Desmond's heart fell to the ground, melting with the snowflakes.

He had to blink a few times to make sure he wasn't

seeing things. But he could only wish it was a hallucination.

Adella was indeed walking through the doors of her hospital. Arm in arm with Wes.

Desmond forced himself forward to greet them.

"Hey, Babe," she said, her body tensing up as soon as she saw his expression. Del pulled her arm from Wes's. "You remember Wes, right? He was coming by to tell me he's getting married."

Desmond didn't know how to feel. Was this the first time she'd seen him in a year? Or did they meet up like this regularly? Behind his back? "He needed to tell you this *why*? And in person... *why*?"

"I didn't mean any disrespect, man," Wes started to explain.

Fighting the snap of his nerves, that they would not whip out in his tone, he replied, "I'm talking to my *wife*."

Adella's gaze deepened. "Baby, we're just clearing the air. He was my friend. And we'd like to be friends again. *All of us*." Adella turned to Wes. "Thanks for stopping by, but he and I should probably talk alone."

Wes gave a respectful nod before he left the two of them.

Desmond didn't know whether to use his humor to dismiss the exchange, or dispense with the polite pretense, and give himself permission to stand in his anger. "The next time I decide to surprise you for lunch, I'll be sure and make an appointment."

He chose the latter.

"That's the first time we've seen each other since that

day you and I met at my house last November. He was just stopping by to give his regards."

His body now a landmine of insecurities and emotions, he said nothing, too afraid he might explode. So, he strolled back to the general parking lot in silence.

"What's been up with you lately?" Adella asked. "Ever since *Dream's* Grand Opening you've been—"

"Do you wish you had married him? Del, if you could have all the same things—the fame, your inheritance, your grandfather's company—but only with *him*, you would never have married me. Do you ever wonder 'what if'? What if you hadn't taken the money? And *me*? A beat-up football player with a piece of a job?" He inhaled the icy air that crawled into him, wrapping around his insides until it froze his heart.

As soon as Desmond saw his words sting her eyes, he wished he hadn't spoken them. But he still meant them.

"Absolutely not. I wish you wouldn't refer to yourself that way. You know you're so much more."

Doubt sat on his shoulders, pushing them back down when he shrugged. "Not how it feels most days. Most days, it feels like I'm not enough. I know it's not your job to prop me up. Only I can do that, baby. I'm not trying to guilt you or anything. It just—"

It hurt. All his youthful fuck-ups. His earlier lack of focus during his teenage years and his twenties. The way he'd partied much of his free time away, when he should have studied more and set himself up for a Plan B. Yet, he had not prepared for his future better. He was too busy being the jock.

Everybody had something, their "thing."

Jerrell had a focus. Desmond's mother had a focus. His brother Keenan was pursuing his passion with *Explore Adventures*. Hell, even his mean-ass sister, Chaitra, was now doing her investment thing.

And though Desmond had a little money left over, some investments, plus his inheritance, he had nothing *real* to show for being Dr. Adella McClain's husband.

So, he would spend the rest of his life confronting every Wes he came across? Every man Adella *should* have married?

Every one of her co-workers, relatives or neighbors who looked at him with a side-eye, wearing a silent question in their expression, of how she wound up with him?

Right then, Desmond shoved his hands in his coat pockets. "I'm not going to the car. I'll just go for a walk." No car heater could warm him now. In fact, the thirties chill may have comforted him just right.

"I thought you came to take me to lunch?" Adella half-asked, half-pleaded.

He had already started walking. Not looking back, he replied, "I lost my appetite."

WHAT ARE YOU DOING?

JERRELL

Nine days before Christmas, Jerrell arrived at the city location of *Poppin' Pauletta's*. But not feeling up to interacting with customers, he entered through the kitchen.

Fortunately, most of the staff were in the front store, along with his grandmother and great-aunt, where he heard clapping and laughing bouncing across the walls. In a foul mood the day before he had to deal with Maddy again, he was in no mood for his grandmother's fussing either. And when Maddy arrived, she'd be staying a week this time for Chrissy's and Sheldon's wedding. The fewer voices he could hear before then, the better.

He squatted to move some boxes closer to the wall and clear a safety hazard. But he twisted his body in a weird way. A cramp rocketed up his back and through his neck.

"Shit!" he muttered.

He grabbed the base of his neck where he started to rub, trying to work out the tension while he rolled his neck around. It had been months since he'd hit the gym or played basketball, and his body was feeling it.

Sheldon had called him about the family going to dinner this evening, and Jerrell was not up for that either. They had just seen each other over Thanksgiving at Sheldon's new house, three weeks before. And they would be seeing each other again at Sheldon's and Chrissy's wedding. Then there was the bachelor party, last minute Christmas shopping, cooking, Christmas Day itself, the hordes of relatives returning to New York from Louisiana. The entire time, he and Maddy would either be treating one another as if the other had lice or sniping back and forth.

Jerrell would not have a moment of peace to himself. Standing and leaning against the stainless steel, he squeezed and massaged the tight cord pulling the nape of his neck, that prevented him from turning his head.

Another set of hands shocked him when they slid over his shoulders and took over the rubbing. Firm, commanding, the thumbs hit in all the right places.

The pressure felt like heaven. He opened his eyes to find one of his newer employees who'd been there a couple of months, Giovanna, standing right next to him. The first place his eyes landed was on her exposed cleavage. Her breasts rose and fell down as her hands worked.

"How is that?" she asked before sucking her lip with intense focus on working out his tension. Her thick, fleshy thighs leaned against him so that her breasts connected with this chest.

"That feels really good actually. Too damn good."

He wanted to tell her to stop. But Maddy hadn't massaged him since before the baby was born. Now Giovanna's magic hands and soft body was easing all the stress. The uptick in his pulse, and alarms ringing in his brain, fired off a warning.

He's right. I don't need him.

Maddy's words chimed in his mind. Along with visions of *Dream's* opening night, how his wife's gaze froze when it landed… over Jerrell's head. On Kevin Middleton.

All thoughts which now toyed with his manhood.

Giovanna's fingers kneaded, working and rubbing, until his tight muscle relaxed, and his head fell lower, toward her breast.

The last time he had seen a rack so mouthwatering—

A violent slap collided with his forehead, sending him backward.

"What are you doing?" A drill sergeant screamed at him. Before Jerrell could focus and see where the last blow came from, another pop sent his head flying back again. "I said *what... are... you doing?*"

The licks flew so fast he didn't have time to see what direction they were coming from.

"You get out of here! Right now!" Gram ordered to Giovanna. When Giovanna headed toward the front of the store, Gram snapped her fingers. "Nah unh, no, Little Girl! You're fired. Get out."

Giovanna's neck popped, "Now wait a minute, Old Lady. This is my rent money. I wasn't even doing anything. Except just standing here. And he asked *me* to help him out. You need to be careful who you snap your fingers at."

Kamilah stepped forward. Only then did Jerrell realize all his siblings were standing in the kitchen, staring at him. And this time, not even Roland was laughing.

"Look, Boo, you're going to be careful who you talk to like that," Kamilah declared. "We will be letting you go with one week severance pay. And if you try any of that sexual-harassment accusation shit, we've got plenty of cameras in here that'll tell the story. If you even try lying, we will send video of your unprofessional conduct to whatever job you get next. So just walk out of here peacefully, and *I'll* stay at peace."

Another whop from Gram's hand sent Jerrell's head to the side, his cramped side that reignited the pain. He clamped his hand against it.

"Damn, Gram! Come on now!"

Yet another whop crashed against his skull. "Did you just curse me? *What* has gotten into you? Boy, the only titties you need to be staring at are the ones that feed your baby!" Gram didn't miss a beat while removing her apron.

"What is your problem? Why have you been coming in here these last few weeks smelling like you live *under* the gutter?"

Jerrell stared at Sheldon, because he had a strong sense Sheldon had already told her. The only other sibling who knew what happened was Kamilah, and she never snitched, no matter what.

"I don't wanna talk about it," Jerrell muttered.

"Yeah, but you gon' talk about it. So, start talkin'. It's Maddy, ain't it? Since you met that girl, the only time you get like this is when you and her are goin' at it. The sky could be fallin', and you wouldn't care, but let Maddy be under it and you lose ya mind."

Jerrell wasn't about to cry.

Especially not in front of Roland. So, he blinked back his pain. Shook his head. Sputtered as he held it in.

As if she could read Jerrell's mind like a novel, Gram waved her hand. "Everybody, out."

Kamila and Etta came to him with hugs, their lips smacking on their little brother's cheek. Sheldon's sermon was etched between his eyebrows, before he turned to follow Roland out. Jerrell could almost hear his older brothers' chastisement to get over himself. And a lot of times, they were probably right. But this situation wasn't so clear. No longer did his life involve just himself.

Once the others left, his grandmother leaned into him, grabbing his chin and shaking it. Her steely eyes were unshaken when they reinforced her words. "Whatever is hanging onto you like this, go to that girl and fix it."

"I wish I could, but I *can't!* That dude, Kevin Middleton, told me—"

"Damn what Kevin Middleton told you!" she snapped, stomping her foot. "You're always letting that boy get in your head. She's *your* wife. Yours."

"You don't know what she did."

The lightning flashed in his grandmother's gray eyes. "And it shouldn't matter now. Weren't y'all doin' just fine before he told you whatever it was?"

"But she doesn't feel like mine anymore." Jerrell pressed his fingers into his eyes, trying to shut out the nightmarish visuals of her using her body to get ahead. "I don't see her the same. When I look at Maddy now, yes, I still love her. I'm still in love with her. But I'm looking at somebody else now. Like I have to learn who she is all over again."

Gram's iron fingers locked onto his face good and tight, so he could look nowhere else but at her. "Well, that's what you'll have to do. You're no damn saint either, in case you forgot all the times you messed around on Raychelle."

At hearing that, Jerrell flinched. He never knew Gram was aware of what happened between him and Ray.

Seeing his reaction, his grandmother scoffed. "Yeah, she called me and cried about what you were doin'." Gram let go of his face, turned her admonishing eyes from him, and spit out her tobacco. "You chose Madison, and she chose *you.* She married *you.* Moved into *your* home. Wears *your* name. Had *your* baby. Not this Middleton boy."

Jerrell shook his head, as if trying to shake out the images of what his wife had done. "You weren't there when Kevin said it. It's like there are three of us in this marriage. I can't enjoy my own wife without something always coming up. Kevin and Maddy are beefing... him and her taking digs at each other... golfing at the same clubs...

hobnobbing in the same circles... I can't catch a damn break. And I wonder if them always fighting is really some secret attraction for each other. On some slick shi... stuff."

Gram's eyes squinted. "Maddy is a powerful woman. Plenty of powerful men will want her. Same way you did. What will you do when she's working for the President? Travelin' on planes with him all the time? You gon' pout about that too?"

Words left him. What *would* he do if she made it all the way to the Oval Office? And he saw even less of her?

Gram's iron finger pointed in front of Jerrell.

"Maddy made her decision about who she wants. I've been around you and her plenty this year. Yeah, she's still uppity. But I see how she looks at you. Whatever mistakes she might have made in the past, she don't come off as the whoring type. So, either you're a man who can stand at her side and love her—*all* of her, weak, strong, good, bad—or you're still just a boy."

His love and admiration for Maddy was a double-edged sword. Exciting, and irritating. Sometimes loving Maddy— her quick, all-consuming mind, all that drive and ego—felt like trying to contain a whirlwind. He could never quite wrap his arms around it.

"That Maddy might be maddening." His grandmother eyed him. "But in some nasty way, it does thangs to you. Man up and own it."

Jerrell hated his grandma knowing him that deeply.

"Now," his grandmother said, switching subjects, "what's this I hear about some Black business meetin'?"

Damn, Shel even told her about that? "Gram, they don't need me, and I don't want to be there with that nig-"

"But you're goin'. My name can't be the only name not in the pot. Whatever they have going on with this *Soul of the Sag*, and with this singer gal, we need to be part of it. Not on the outside lookin' in. So, pick up your lip and get it done."

Jerrell protested, "My business is doing fine. I don't need that dude."

His grandmother returned a clear-eyed gaze to her grandson. "What's the matter? Can't look him in the eye?"

"Of course, I can. But I want to punch him every time I do."

"Is this about him and Maddy, or him and *you*? You jealous because he's got money?" Gram asked.

The stoves may as well have been firing in his chest, shooting flames into his eye sockets.

So he might have envied Kevin a little. And wondered if Maddy carried regrets about her choice.

"Do you see all this here?" Gram continued, spreading her arms. "This is all you. You're not some spoiled rich kid. You didn't have everything handed to ya. You worked your butt off for this. Yeah, you got a little help when you needed it. But you didn't have no silver spoon or no blank check. Hold your head up. And when you go see this Middleton meddler, you will look him right in his eye. It won't matter that he's the richer man. You're the better man. Maddy married the *better* man."

"Where's my mama?" a gruff male voice echoed from the front of the store. The kitchen door burst open. Jerrell grunted when he saw his father standing inside it. Along with Jerrell's siblings in tow. "I know y'all didn't think you were going out to eat with my mama and I wasn't coming."

Kamila reached out and grabbed Jerrell's neck. He flinched at the sloppy kiss she planted on his cheek. "Love you, Bro."

As always, his dad walked around the kitchen like he owned the place, even though this was none of his establishment. Moving from pan to pan, Charles Rouse popped various morsels in his mouth.

"Mmm." He popped in a few more samples. "Ooh!"

Until he finally made his way around to his youngest son.

Jerrell rolled his eyes when his father stopped in front of him.

"I was about to knock some sense into ya." He slapped the crumbs off his fingers. "But I can see from your face she already handled it."

DEZZY DOG

DESMOND

*I*nstead of driving home, back in Boston, Desmond had boarded a quick flight back to the Hamptons.

To put a little space between him and Del, he went to see his brother Keenan at *Explore Adventures.*

He entered the little guest center on Main Street, where vacationers arrived for their weekend breaks from New York City.

Desmond's heart filled with pride at what his little brother had accomplished in such a short time.

Within less than a year, Keenan had brought together four charismatic, powerful black men to revolutionize Black travel and adventure. Desmond was proud that, all over America, socialites and professionals were talking about the "Black Luxury Guys." The "Black Travelists," the "Black Frontiersmen"—guys forging the way ahead, in futurism and globalism. And the banks and big-name corporations were all in, because they already understood the value of black dollars.

Rather than going to movie theaters, and splurging on theme parks, Black people were getting on yachts and saving their coins for innovative experiences. Keenan had even managed to reel in the indomitable Kevin Middleton.

Right now, Keenan was busy giving directions to *Explore's* concierge, Laney. Desmond suspected this boy was also giving her something else on the side too.

"These eleven couples here are also top investors in *Explore,* so let's make sure when they arrive, we have our premium care baskets put together and complementary dinners are laid out nicely over at *Taste.* Make sure that Miracle gets this order. Those guests also receive discounts at *Oasis Cove Hotel.* Oh! And inform Solomon of when they get here. I've got to fly to Baltimore, but Solomon should be present to greet them personally," Keenan instructed her.

"Sure thing," Laney replied. She lingered at the door before heading back out to the front desk. "And about… our meeting later?"

Keenan shot a glance at Desmond, who bit back a laugh.

Keenan cleared his throat. "Yes, um, we'll discuss those spring bookings before we close."

"Spring bookings, huh?" Desmond asked, snort-laughing while he reached onto the tiny back-office desk for a wrapped, chocolate candy filled with liquor and labeled *Taste the Love*. "How many bookings she got up in that cooch?"

His little brother smacked his lips. "Dude, shut up. Your ass is no better than me. The only reason you behave now is because Mama made you marry Adella. And Del's got so much clout you'd be screwed if you screw her over."

The older brother ignored that last comment about his wife's importance. As if he needed to be reminded. "So, what are you saying? It's time for Mama to make you man up and marry Ilyana? Or will you just keep screwing her in the back of the brewery?"

Desmond burst out laughing harder as his brother's face melted.

"How did you know that? That shit's not funny," Keenan said, throwing a chocolate candy at his big brother.

Desmond's gut kept shaking. "A little bird told me."

"You mean Martin's trifling ass told his sister Adella, and she told you to come and talk to me."

Desmond shrugged. "Dude, what did I tell you about this whole Ilyana situation? If you don't plan to lock her down, leave it alone. Our families are already tied up in a mess as it is. And here you go, banging my wife's little sister while you're trying to work out these kinks with *Dream Stage*? Do you really think that's helping anything? You're a good businessman, *except* when it comes to your dick."

"I can't help that Ilyana was chasing my shit like a piranha."

"Oh, you couldn't throw her off, huh?"

"If she wants to suck like that, who am I to deny her? Do you hear her complaining? Everybody else is complaining. But Ilyana's not complaining. So, what's the problem?" Keenan asked in all seriousness, popping a candy in his mouth. "Anyway, what happened with Jerrell?"

Desmond shook his head. "He's not doing it. I tried."

"Try harder. We all need him to come in. And as much as I hate her ass, we need Maddy in this Business Council thing. *Explore* is doing nicely, with all our national publicity. But some of these local folks won't deal with us. They still handle us like outsiders, because they're loyal to Maddy and Chrissy. I still can't get into that damn country club. I've got Kevin's endorsement, but I need more. Maddy won't come without Jerrell."

"And Jerrell hates Kevin, who's your partner now. So game over."

Keenan threw up his arms and scoffed. "That dude can't keep acting like a damn douche though. We're all grown. None of us likes this, but we've all got to suck it up, so we can all make money next year."

Desmond shifted subjects, to the foremost reason he came—his future. "Have you thought about that position?

Working with Martin at *Slurp*? I've got my money lined up."

Keenan also shifted, seeming to detect the change of his older brother's mood. "What's up with you, man? I thought you were supposed to be back in Boston with Del. All of a sudden, you swoop in here again? What *happened?*"

Desmond rolled his eyes, refusing to admit that he'd seen Wes. And that it lit a new fire under his management pursuits. "All your hard work is taking off. You're having a damn good time, making me want a piece of the action. We could work with each other. Just like Solomon and Martin."

With the long, ugly inhale he took, Keenan may as well have been smoking from a chimney.

"Are you seriously ready, bruh? I know you're my brother and everything, and you've almost got the MBA, but Martin has executive experience helping Solomon run their real estate company. Every man in our partnership has led a company or a division. This *Explore* set-up is my baby, man."

"I know, I know. The brewery where I'm working now will vouch for me. They already offered me an assistant manager position. But I want to do this thing with you. So, what's up? Why do you keep giving me the run-around, man?"

Keenan's hand wiped down his face. "You've never been a dealmaker, Dezzy. You've always been Dezzy Dog. Chaitra and I had to do the heavy lifting for *McLain Construction*. While you showed up and..."

Desmond could tell his little brother was searching for

the nicest way to describe his whoring, so he helped him out. "Smiled for the cameras."

Keenan sighed. "That's one way of phrasing it." He scooted off his desk. "All of these guys put in work. Kevin is a damn walking thirst trap, with his own Los Angeles tech company, and he even puts in elbow grease for *Explore*. This isn't like back at *McLain Construction*, when you could hide somewhere and drink half the day. We're in the trenches now. The world is watching us Black men. Mostly waiting for us to fuck up."

Desmond winced at the reminder of his old ways. "Look, I get it. I understand. I have a lot of proving to do. And I can't just coast on my football player rep the way I used to. Give me a chance, Lil Bro. Back then, I didn't have a wife giving me a sense of purpose."

Keenan's eyebrow cocked up with his skepticism. "You mean making your sorry ass look bad while she works hard."

"Okay, yeah, that too." The two brothers doubled over chuckling. "But I like this brewery shit. It's the first thing I've ever really been interested in. I've visited several, learned the processes, tasted the difference between brews of corn and rice versus barley, and how long they sit in the tanks. The flavors and how to achieve them. I've even whipped up some ideas."

"What makes your ideas any better than Martin's?"

Desmond inhaled. "He might be a businessman, but I don't believe he wants to do this."

Keenan's back stiffened. "What makes you think that?"

"He was over at the house this weekend talking to

Adella about their granddad's real estate company. He acts like he misses it."

Keenan shrugged. "Big deal. It's their family business. Of course, he probably misses being around his people, and the way things used to be when his granddaddy was alive. Hell, if my money train was gone, I would miss it too."

Desmond thought fast. "But is that what you want on your team? Somebody who's only got one foot in and one foot out? Is he innovating *Slurp's* offerings and customer experience? Or is he just babysitting what you've already got in place?" The older brother rubbed his hands together. "You know if anybody can show folks a good time and bring that drink game, it's me."

He could tell from Keenan's silence, and the way Little Bro gritted his teeth, that he'd put something on Keenan's mind.

Desmond continued, "If you do wind up losing Martin, and I was already in position, you wouldn't have to shop around for somebody new. You would have a guy ready to go who knows the ropes."

"I'd have to get buy-in from the others. Complete your MBA, and we'll talk. Besides, how will you do this when you and Adella live in Boston mostly?"

"Now that we're trying for a family, and she's got *Dream Stage*, we're thinking of switching it up and spending time mostly in New York. Her closest friends are here, and it's where Del feels most comfortable. She wants our kids to grow up with Maddy's and Chrissy's. And I know Del won't admit it, but even though she and her brothers are still beefing, Martin and Solomon are here. Ilyana comes through a lot to hang with Cher. Del wants to be closer to all of them."

Keenan nodded his understanding. "All right then. But your request to join us will get a lot more support with the boys, if you bring in Jerrell.

Desmond winced. It was a tall order. "Jerrell hates half of y'all."

"At least get him out of our way. These folks around here respect him. And *Explore's* not going anywhere. So, we may as well move on. You help convince him of that, and it'll be easier for me to convince the fellas to bring you in."

ON YOUR KNEES

MADDY, JERRELL & CHRISSY

MADDY

Thirty minutes after waking, Maddy still lay in bed. Chase hadn't awakened. Darkness still shrouded her bedroom.

Later this afternoon, she would head back to Sag Harbor. To Jerrell.

And try to power through the way her husband looked at her now, since the meeting with Kevin.

Burying her face in her pillow, she wet it with her tears. The last time he was here, her womanhood had ached so bad for him to make love to her. To tower over her, while he filled her up, for his body to cover hers like he owned her. Instead, he'd slept on the couch. And she didn't dare go to him again, and attempt to reconcile, only to catch his coldness in another silent rejection.

Somewhere on her bed, her phone buzzed. She prayed it wasn't Jerrell wanting to see Chase, or her mother or sister asking irritating questions in an effort to analyze or critique her.

Adella: *You sure you really are going through with this?*

They'd had a crying session over the phone the night before.

Maddy: *Yes, I'm going through with it. I'm not happy anymore. Things have changed. Time to move on.*

Adella: *I'll be rooting for you.*

Maddy chuckled, wiping away more tears. *And I'm screaming for you to get pregnant with triplets.*

Two hours later, she'd fed Chase and the nanny had arrived. She'd spent the week putting together their luggage for the week-long excursion in New York. They would start off in Sag Harbor so she could knock out some paperwork at *Dream Stage*. Jerrell would check in on that location of *Poppin Pauletta's*, and they would hit some of the social events with the baby. After a few days, they would head to New York City for a couple of days, and then to Alpine.

It used to be that she would put on her game face for her job. Now Maddy required armor for her employer *and* her husband. Both of her jobs.

How they would pull off this farce of being the giddy newlyweds, she had no clue.

Never in her life had she wanted to fuck and strangle somebody at the same time.

Riding through the streets of D.C., on the way to the office, she stared at the slate gray sky. Even when the sun shined now on Capitol Hill, the place was still gray.

Barricades lined the streets, walling off parking lots and walkways that were once open. Stepping out of the car, she averted her eyes from the protestors shouting one another down across Pennsylvania Avenue.

"Come on, folks! Keep it moving!" the police officer demanded once his eyes shifted up and down, from her face to her Capitol Hill identification badge.

Rushing to get in the building, she moved through several sets of metal detectors and more police, who now barked at staffers, motioning them along as if they were cattle.

A few of the staffers she once chatted with so easily, regardless of what party they served, now met her eyes in the marble halls and kept walking. Much of their new iciness was due to the new social and political divide in America.

However, some of their frost was due to them learning Maddy had money.

She could often tell the difference. People who were curious about her wealth would stare a little longer, give her a once-over and evaluate her appearance for signs of excess.

But today, when she crossed paths with her colleagues from the other side of the aisle, the vibe felt… weird.

One of them glanced at her, accompanied with a sort of smirk, before he looked away. Another colleague suppressed a tiny smile.

Whatever. She would manage these next few short hours, and then, she would be out of here. For the morning, she sent out a couple of memos, and accompanied her Virginia Senator and boss to a Senate foreign trade hearing regarding the supply chain backups at ports across America. Having answers ready for him and snapping to his side at the drop of a dime wasn't as easy as it used to be.

Her thoughts kept meandering back to Jerrell. On her mind were Chase's soft whimpers as she turned him over to the nanny that morning.

Her eyes blinked back a fresh wave of tears. She was determined not to cave, not to give her colleagues a spectacle. Not after all the years she'd stood strong.

Only when she captured a glimpse of her bare, exhausted face in one of the television monitors did she realize she hadn't put on makeup.

Shock flew through Maddy. A long, black stick pointed straight at her. Right down the middle of it was a hole.

A small tunnel.

A gun barrel.

And then a blast of fire.

Blood splattered against her face.

Screams stormed her ears. Bodies bolted. Maddy spent around in her seat, to Senator Easton, who blinked in bewilderment next to her. He touched his hand to the bloody hole in his upper chest. Another staffer tackled him, pushing him to the floor. Another bullet busted into his seat. Maddy quickly dived from her own chair.

"Everybody, get your hands in the air where we can see 'em!" the camera operator's jaws wagged. "We're taking back our government!"

JERRELL

"Get out of here," Jerrell said to Chrissy with a laugh. "Stop shitting me."

"Nope. I really was in that rap video. To this day, my parents have no idea," Chrissy replied, chuckling while holding her belly.

Jerrell couldn't stop rolling with laughter as they rode down the freeway. "Does Sheldon know?"

Smiling that big, gorgeous grin of hers, she shook her head. "No. And if you tell him, I'll deny it."

They both cracked up.

"But you know Shel probably already knows, right?

Hell, with all that tech shit he does, he's hacked into every-body and their damn dog," Jerrell said laughingly.

Chrissy winked as they arrived at their destination. "Your brother can investigate all he wants. He's not going anywhere. I make sure of *that*."

Jerrell cringed at the thought of Sheldon having sex. "Ew!"

They kept guffawing. The two of them were attending Pastor Arnold's first Black Business Council meeting, she on behalf of *Dream Stage*, and he for *Poppin' Pauletta's*.

They had ridden in from the city together. Though Chrissy was also born and bred in New York polite society, she could have easily been a hood chick. As much as she loved dancing, rap music, and hip-hop culture, she could have grown up in the Bronx.

Jerrell laughed at her stories of going to concerts, chasing rappers and trying to sneak onto video sets when she was supposed to be at the mall. He could see why Sheldon loved her. Her flirty, adventurous spirit was perfectly suited for his restless older brother who got bored easily.

The ride hadn't been awkward, despite Jerrell and his wife having tension. Maddy was Chrissy's close childhood friend, but during this ride, they hadn't discussed Maddy once. The conversation had been all shits and giggles.

"Ready?" Chrissy asked Jerrell, when they stood at the entrance to a conference room at the *Oasis Cove Hotel*.

"As I'll ever be," he replied with a scowl, trying his best to straighten up his face.

"We'll face him down together," she muttered before they entered.

A handful of the Hamptons Black business-owners all shook hands. The owners of *Sharon's* restaurant, *Cal's* sports bar, *Explore Adventures*, a couple of clothing boutiques, a candy store, all amounted to about fourteen business-owners.

Jerrell's handshake with Kevin, and his partner Keenan, was firm and stiff. Jaws locked, eye contact forced, it all lasted about three seconds before the three men parted ways. The others were joined by Adella's brother, Solomon English, the co-owner and operator of *Taste*, her other brother Martin English, the co-owner and operator of *Slurp*, and Roccard Giacchino, the co-owner and operator of *Explore*.

Pastor Arnold started the meeting.

"Seeing this fellowship is a real blessing. A first step in restoring civility, respect, and one shared purpose among families and neighbors. I thank you all for taking time from your busy schedules to join us today."

They got into the nuts and bolts of the next year's schedule—*Explore's* major events, the schedule for *Dream Stage, Poppin' Pauletta's* ability to cater, promotions of *Sharon's* and *Taste*, as well as *Cal's*, and supporting one another.

"Uh, excuse us a moment," Pastor Arnold said, as his assistant pushed her phone in front of him.

While the Pastor did that, Jerrell got up to grab coffee he'd been too distracted to pour at the beginning of the meeting. It would also give him a tiny break from looking at Kevin Middleton's face for two hours.

Jerrell stirred in a little sugar, took a sip.

When he turned around, the entire room was staring at him.

On the table, his phone lit up, buzzing insistently.

Chrissy's normally caramel-tinted skin had turned near-green, as if she may have stopped breathing.

He looked at his phone and read a news alert.

Several gunmen posing as camera operators have taken hostages at the Capitol.

Frantic text messages followed.

Before he knew it, his hand and pants leg were burning. His coffee cup lay empty on the floor.

Voices spoke somewhere in the ether.

With tears blinding him, his limbs going numb, Jerrell felt as if a gunman had just shot him. Unable to feel or see or identify anything or anybody, he was already stumbling out the door.

CHRISSY

"How soon will a jet be available?" Chrissy asked Sheldon over the phone.

"Not until tonight. Can somebody drive him to the city so he can fly out from LaGuardia?"

"Traffic will be a nightmare. He may as well wait," Chrissy said, staring at a distraught Jerrell who quietly cried while on the phone with Maddy's parents. They were already taking a helicopter from Virginia to D.C.

Murmurs swirled around them, while on the other end of the phone, Sheldon tried to figure out an alternative.

In Chrissy's peripheral vision, Pastor Arnold was talking to Keenan McClain.

"Can you fly him, son?" the Pastor asked.

Chrissy had forgotten that Keenan possessed his pilot's license, but she'd been convinced it was mostly for bragging rights.

"I can't," Keenan said. "I'm already scheduled to leave for Baltimore after this meeting, to attend to our construction company. I've delayed that building demolition several times. The city will fine my mother's construction company if we delay again. *Explore's* biggest investors are flying in here tonight, and I can't even be present for them."

The business-owners began to pray, a couple of them long time neighbors of Maddy's grandmother, who got on their knees.

Chrissy squeezed Jerrell's shaking shoulders, while his head was a bowling ball in his hand.

"I'll take him."

Everyone turned around.

Jerrell lifted his eyes.

Chrissy had completely forgotten that Kevin had his pilot's license.

Now the two men faced only one another. Kevin's red-eyed face seemed to reflect Jerrell's horror.

But Kevin walked forward. "I'll cancel the rest of my day. And fly him to his wife."

JERRELL

Is the real asshole the person who pretends she's some smart, self-sufficient diva when really all she is is a hoe?

Jerrell's words now knifed the folds of his brain. Slashed his thoughts.

All televisions displayed the news alerts and field reporters, but they provided no real news.

Phone calls to the Senator's office gave a busy signal. Chrissy's hasty fingers dialed the U.S. Capitol operator. She tried other Senate offices, as well as Maddy's other colleagues and friends. With the few responses she received, other staffers and other Senate rooms didn't know what was happening.

The last images replaying in Jerrell's mind were of blood splattering his wife's face. Terrified employees screamed. Their bodies hit the floor.

No news on how many were dead, or how many were alive. Or who.

Other than his daily video calls to see Chase, his last words to her had been agreement that he wished he'd never married her. Those had been her last words to him.

Would he ever get to tell her it couldn't have been further from the truth?

Sitting on the bench, his head almost left his neck when it collapsed to his chest.

His Maddy Cakes.

He had been so stupid.

On camera, gunmen had overtaken the Senate hearing room, right before the networks shut down the live feed. The President issued a directive ordering news stations to stop broadcasting, to avoid a public execution that could give the attackers leverage, or some perceived power to negotiate.

But Jerrell desperately wished to see, to breathe again. To know that his *wife* still breathed.

"J?" Chrissy's voice brought him back from the swamp of anguish.

He lifted his head from his hands.

When he stared up, staring back at him was Kevin Middleton.

What the hell did this dude want?

Jerrell did not have the strength or headspace to ask.

Kevin spoke, "I've got a friend over at Southampton Heliport who can cancel one of his flights; he'll let me borrow his helicopter. If we get there in the next few minutes, I can have you in D.C. in the next two hours."

A flicker of light must have passed through Jerrell's heart. Seeing only his wife's face, and nothing else, the vision must have been his guiding light. It gave him the energy to nod.

He didn't care if the Grinch came and rode him to D.C., or even Satan himself. All that mattered right now was getting to their son as soon as possible, and then getting to his wife.

Though somewhere around him, he heard and felt the support of others patting his back, squeezing his shoulders and arms, he wasn't present.

His mind, senses, feelings were all hundreds of miles away, with his family. He hardly noticed when he was riding in the back of an SUV, mere inches separating him and Kevin.

Neither man spoke. Silence enshrouded Jerrell while he stared out the window at a platinum, emotionless sheet of sky.

Kevin's big security escort accompanied them to a helicopter, its rotor blades turning.

Jerrell slid into the backseat. Kevin and his security took to the front seats.

Kevin took the pilot's chair, which surprised Jerrell. He had thought Kevin was renting a helicopter for someone else to pilot.

A silent question crossed Jerrell's mind, but his humble gratitude kept him silent.

As they took off and flew over Sag Harbor, and then Montauk, Kevin operated the control panels and gears like it was second nature.

The occasional dialogue between Kevin and his security detail was ambient noise to Jerrell. The rotors beat against the wind, and they flew down the coastline.

Jerrell had taken this journey South plenty of times over the past few weeks, making numerous trips back-and-forth to be with his wife and son. Now the once scenic views may as well have been black.

He wiped a tear. With a stifled sob, he hoped and prayed that his heart and better half would be in his arms again. That she would know how precious she was to him, and that he would have no life without her.

The Lord is my Shepherd.

I shall not w...

His fingers mashed his eyes, rubbing the tears into his skin.

Please Lord, give me another chance.

Please forgive me for taking my blessings for granted.

Jerrell had already lost one angel God placed in his life. As his grandmother aptly pointed out.

What if he had lost another?

Two hours later, Jerrell breathed a sigh of relief that he was finally at least in the same city with his family.

Kevin landed the helicopter at the heliport closest to the U.S. Capitol.

Wracked with worry, Jerrell couldn't unbuckle the seatbelt fast enough. His fingers fumbled at the door latch to throw it open. Kevin's security guard helped him out.

The entire ride, Jerrell had said nothing, too busy praying, running every possible scenario through his mind, and ringing his hands. But before making his exit, he froze.

He turned and peered over his shoulder.

Kevin was already looking over his.

With no words, the two men eyed one another.

Jerrell acknowledged him with a head nod.

With a slight bow, Kevin bid him well.

MADDY

He's right. I don't need him.

Would she ever get to tell her husband how her clit twitched when he slid his arm around her? How she missed waking up to his leg thrown over her, his morning log embedded in her thigh? The way her pulse sped up or her pussy leaked in her panties when his mouth was coming toward her. Or when he looked at her like he was ready to eat.

Would they ever have one of those intimate, quiet moments again? Since she had gotten pregnant with Chase early in their relationship, they had only taken two trips together. To Mexico and Cape Cod. But they never stayed long, so he could get back to his new business, and she could return to juggling her job with helping Chrissy's and Adella's new ventures.

Now would they get to travel, see the world, make love on the beach again? Would she feel like the safest, most secure woman on the planet?

"Get on your knees! On your knees!" The screaming cameramen and television crew held homemade weapons over their heads.

Senator Easton had been shot but was still breathing. Eight Senators lay along the wall with him, while their captors yelled out threats.

It was apparent this was a planned operation, that these guys had slowly smuggled in simple wooden and plastic parts over a matter of weeks or months, one item at a time.

Now, the men removed their shoes, necklaces, and belts. They opened tiny containers and clasps and constructed weaponry, as if they had spent years preparing for war. They had compiled makeshift guns from undetectable pieces smuggled in, bit by bit. Primers, springs, and triggers, had all been snuck into secret compartments built into their cameras, belt buckles, and steel-toed boots.

"Put your cell phones in this box! No talking. Stop whining! This is for your country!" a woman screamed.

Maddy searched the floor for her cellphone. The last call she saw coming through was Adella. Maddy quickly activated her FaceTime feature before giving up her phone. She dropped it facedown in the bucket, so her phone was on and Adella could record whatever she heard on the other end.

Staffers crouched together, steeling themselves and putting on determined faces.

"Stand down! Now!" Military officers shouted on the other side of the door that had been barred shut with long metal curtain rods and furniture.

The captors shouted back. "Until the President gives up his office, we will execute a hostage every hour! This is a declaration of war! We are taking back Am—"

A blast jolted Maddy where she lay on the ground.

"Heads down! Everybody, cover your heads! Now!" a man screamed.

Maddy buried her head under her arms, scooting under the chairs as gunfire rained from the ceiling. Canisters rolled into the fallen doors and through scattered chairs, blanketing the room with gray smoke. More gunfire sprayed from the cameramen.

"I've got a hostage! I'll kill her! Not another step!"

One of Maddy's colleagues cried, begging them not to kill her.

More shots blared.

Boots pounded the carpet, but Maddy could not see who they were. If they were more terrorists, or police coming to save them.

"Down! Down! On the floor! Lay down!"

"Put it down! Put it down!"

"I will never surrender!"

"Put the gun *down*!"

"You'll have to take it from my cold, dead--"

Deft, targeted shots whipped over their heads.

Shielding her head with only her arms, Maddy prayed Chase would clutch her breast again.

Prayed she would walk him into his first day of school.

Prayed she would live to tell Jerrell she couldn't think straight without him.

DADDY

MADDY & JERRELL

MADDY

*B*odies smushed together like sardines, Maddy and her colleagues cowered behind the hearing benches.

A dreadfully long silence engulfed the room.

Maddy lifted a finger from her eye to peek. Through the smoke, she could barely make out the door. There, military officers crouched. One of them looked straight at her and placed a quieting index finger over his mouth. They now appeared to be searching the room with guns drawn.

They had begun making arrests. One of the officers finally lifted his walkie-talkie to his mouth. "We've got clean visuals now. Situation is stabilized. All living suspects are detained. Three are deceased. No others in view. Are we clear to move hostages out?"

Three hours after the first shot was fired, the sweetest words Maddy could've heard were, "All right, come on, folks. Let's get you out of here."

Army soldiers swept an arm under the staffers to help them off the floor.

"Have you been hurt, ma'am? Shot?" A Black soldier swept his arm around her waist, pulling her to him a little close. But there was only one pair of arms she longed to feel.

Once taken to a makeshift medical area with ambulances, she was checked for injuries. The dried blood on her blouse was Senator Easton's, and thankfully, he was still alive.

After medical clearances, soldier escorts guided staffers through the elaborate, ornate hallways she once loved. Right now, she wanted nothing more than to leave.

That morning, she had turned in her two weeks' notice.

The Senator had asked her to hold off and wait, to help him with his White House run for president in a couple of years. He'd said he would need her expertise concerning the pressures of foreign trade, supply chains, and the impact on struggling American small businesses.

A year ago, she would have. But Maddy was a different woman now. Same drive, same ambition. Different priorities.

After helping Adella and Chrissy earlier that year, watching both of them take off, knowing all the possibilities that lay before her, Maddy had developed an appetite for a new way of using her skills.

"The cameraman told me to get on the ground and shots were fired. Blood hit me. The Senator was wounded Her brain moved in and out of a fog as she gave her initial interview to investigators.

Hard as she tried to recall them, the events had exploded so fast she barely remembered. A few precious, fleeting seconds, just a few more inches, and those bullets could've ended Maddy.

She was not invincible. She would not have forever to appreciate the little things.

Finally, after another several hours of being questioned and interviewed by police and FBI authorities, soldiers escorted staffers out of the building, into waiting vehicles. They were driven to a hotel a short distance away, where her colleagues were running inside.

Her legs shaking, Maddy stumbled from the SUV, and searched the numerous faces.

Only now did she notice one of her shoes was gone. But she hobbled forward, watching her co-workers run into the arms of spouses and parents.

Where were hers?

JERRELL

The cops still had provided no information.

Secret Service agents were tight-lipped and evasive with answers, giving no details.

Relatives had been corralled into a hotel conference room down the street from the Capitol to await word of their loved ones' safety during the standoff. Parents and spouses spouted off one question after another.

Jerrell had no idea or clue of how many were alive, or dead. Maddy's parents paced the floors with him. At times holding hands or hugging, they tried to reassure one another she would be fine.

"I said things I shouldn't have said, Dr. Page," he admitted to Maddy's father.

Dr. Page offered a tortured half-grin. "That's marriage, son. My daughter knows your true heart. It's clear every time I see the two of you together."

In anguish, Jerrell's head swung from side to side. "It's not the same. I shouldn't have talked to my baby that way."

He sobbed while squeezing his head. "God blessed me with another chance at love, and I screwed it up

The pressure of Dr. Page's hand at his neck was of little comfort. "If you didn't love her, you would not have said anything at all. And Maddy is smart enough to know that. God is with her. Her grandmother Estaire is with her. C-covering he…" But even as he said it, Dr. Page choked up.

Jerrell wiped his own eyes.

Finally, cars began pulling into the circular driveway outside. Families rushed out the door to greet Capitol Hill employees before the cars stopped.

None of them were Maddy.

"Oh, God! Oh, my God!" Jerrell called, searching faces. "Where is she?"

"She's coming," her mother muttered. "My baby girl is a fighter. There's no way she won't survive," Mrs. Page said as her own eyes scanned.

They kept surveying all the heads and bodies.

Jerrell's noodle-soft bones barely allowed him to stand. He crumbled, nailing his hands to his knees when she still hadn't appeared.

A handful of desperate families still waited, their eyes darting with no answers. They held out hope in the dark.

Through his tears, a pair of legs came toward him.

Her mother's scream filled the air. "Praise God!"

Her parents grabbed her, kissing her and crying. Jerrell could barely stand.

Maddy walked toward him. He could only fling his arms around her knees.

His wife sank to the ground, and he felt the precious

skin to skin of the one person whose touch now gave him life.

"Baby, I'm so—" he sobbed, hyperventilating. His tongue was paralyzed.

"I love you, Baby," his angel spoke the only words he wanted to hear. "I'm sorry you found out that way."

"Nnn… I'm so sorry. I'm so fucking sorry for how I talk —" was all he could manage. He gathered the strength to stand and scoop her up. Took her to a waiting car that transported them home.

Maddy's parents made the calls to the rest of the family. They passed the phone around to Jerrell's parents in New York, and then Chrissy and Sheldon, as well as to Maddy's siblings and other relatives. Numerous other calls came in, until Jerrell turned off their phones.

While her mom prepared dinner, Jerrell started the shower, so Maddy could wash off the dry blood.

When he turned to her, his stormy little wife had entered a mental fog.

Teetering on the edge of the toilet seat, she hallucinated. Jerking, she swatted at a vision only she saw. With a flinch of her eyes, the tightening of her face, she dodged from sounds only she heard.

Slamming her eyes, Maddy shut out the world. Tears seeped through her eyelids. A small earthquake jarred her slender frame as she broke down crying.

A desperate Jerrell thudded to the floor at her side.

"Babe," he whispered, hating to see his strong, defiant girl this way. His forehead collapsed against hers. "Maddy Cakes."

Like a mechanical robot, her head swiveled from side to

side, and she seemed to be slipping back to the atrocity she'd endured.

"Maddy Cakes. *No.* Come back, baby. Don't leave me. We need you. Chase needs you. I need you. You're the strongest person I know. Look at *me*," Jerrell coaxed, giving her a tiny shake.

Her eyes crept open. He slid his fingers under his baby's chin, holding it up to maintain eye contact with her, and to ensure the light didn't dim inside her.

Jerrell peeled off her clothes, with no regard for his, and lifted her into the shower. He sat her in the chair she used when she was pregnant and washed her. Moving the soapy sponge over her feet, he lifted each one, planting several kisses on each foot. Occasionally, his eyes snapped to hers, to keep her attention, so she didn't drift back to her state of shock.

After drying her off and moisturizing her the way she liked, he placed her in pajamas.

Still silent, his girl was at least holding onto him now. Almost as if sharing the strain of her horror, her head tipped onto his shoulder. Laying his lips in her hair, he stroked and gripped it, over and over. His soft reassurances blended with the crackling flames from the fireplace. "I'm here, baby. You're not alone."

Slowly pulling away, he rose to get Chase and bring the baby to her.

"I lied."

His wife's voice stopped Jerrell at the door. He spun around to find her gazing at him.

"When I said I didn't need you," she finished.

With no hesitation, he moved to the bed and kneeled. "I shouldn't have treated you like that, baby."

Their eyes finally, truly connected. Seeing life in Maddy released the chokehold around his lungs.

"It didn't happen the way Kevin said, and he was just gaslighting. Dr. Messenger—"

Jerrell grabbed the side of her face. "I don't care. You've done phenomenal things, you help the world, and you're mine, and I'm damn proud of you."

Their cries stifled the apologies, until they were sobbing and clinging. And silently digesting how close they'd come to never being able to apologize. All that interrupted their reunion was the sound of their son waking up in the next room.

He watched Maddy wipe away tears as she sat in her grandmother's rocking chair. When he handed her their son, she kissed the hands of the tiny child in her arms and started to breastfeed him.

"I quit my job today," she murmured.

Her parents stopped eating.

A flood of joy broke the dam across Jerrell's heart, though he didn't want it to. He knew how much she loved politics and Washington, D.C.

"Baby, don't give up your dreams." It wasn't what he wanted to say. But he would support her goals. "Your career means everything to you. We'll just be more coordinated and patient with each—"

"I'm not giving up anything. You and Chase are part of my dream. My dreams look different now." She didn't turn her eyes from where their son lay in her arms. Her feet kept tapping the floor, rocking back and forth. She was calm, resolute, as if the events of today had taken her some place the rest of them could not go.

From that furnace of hatred and violence today, she seemed to have emerged made of tougher steel.

MADDY

A knock at the bedroom door the next morning pulled Maddy from the sleep she was finally getting. The night had been restless, as she shook off attackers demanding that she, *Get on your knees!*

On top of her, Jerrell lay with his head in her neck, his arm tightly locked around her, as if that were his way of shielding her. His morning tree was growing into her butt cheek.

"Babe," she whispered underneath him, before he woke up.

Even then, he still hesitated to withdraw from her. Finally, he got up. At the door were Maddy's parents, who were leaving.

"We're going to head out, but we'll see you in Sag Harbor tomorrow?" her mother asked.

"Yes, ma'am," Jerrell said.

Her father appeared and the two men walked out to the hallway.

Maddy's mother came toward her for a hug, leaning against her ear. "He was losing his mind over you." Her mother squeezed her tighter. "We all were. Whatever you two said or did, let this be a lesson."

The two women held on a little longer before letting each other go. "I love you, Baby."

"I love you too, Mommy," Maddy said, before her mother headed to the baby's crib, laying a kiss on Chase, and then hugged Jerrell on the way out.

"Yes, Sir," she overheard Jerrell saying to her father in the foyer. Both men's voices seemed serious but grateful.

Moving slower, allowing herself to appreciate that she was alive to turn on the bathroom light, she wiped a couple more grateful tears and started her morning routine.

While bent over scrubbing her skin, pressure bumped against her ass, an insistent pressure she hadn't felt since before the baby was born.

Even with remnants of fear and uncertainty hiding inside her, she smiled at the familiar feeling she missed.

He leaned over her and his hands joined hers as she shut off the water knob. His strong arms wrapped her inside them. And he tucked his face in her shoulder, staring at her in the mirror. "We'll survive it together."

Seeing the men's faces again, staring down the barrel of the gun, knowing it would shoot her next, Maddy retreated behind her eyelids.

"No," Jerrell said, turning her around and nuzzling her face with his. "Baby, open your eyes."

Maddy forced her gaze to his. Her husband was as handsome as ever.

His smooth lips started at hers. Glided to her cheek, then her temple. To her forehead, and then her nose. Who would have thought simple kisses could ease so much mental strain? Especially from the right mouth. Jerrell's fingers pulled at the drawstring of her pajama bottoms.

He seemed to hesitate. Like he was still grappling with something but working his way through it.

"Kevin and I never had sex, Jerrell." She braced herself for this conversation she knew they needed. To give him the answers she knew *he* needed. "But he did ask me to marry him."

Jerrell's eyes mountain-climbed to hers. His jaw tightened, but finally, he let her talk.

"The night of the Turners' *Ivory* gala back in January, right before you came up to the balcony. When you heard me say, 'I wouldn't let him hurt you.' You wanted to know how he could hurt you."

Her husband blinked a moment, as he seemed to recall that night.

Maddy continued, "He offered to raise my baby as his own son." She watched Jerrell's eyes almost bulge from his head. "Kevin was concerned I was damaging my reputation by having a baby out of wedlock. I think he was trying to be an honorable man, maybe make up for his wrongs by helping me. But I loved you, J. And when I told Kevin no, I didn't know how the future looked for you and me. But I knew my future wasn't him."

Maddy slid her hand inside Jerrell's, and let her mind return to her childhood.

"I do envy Kevin though. I always wanted to be him. For as long as I can remember, he was always king, ruler of the world." She swiped another tear. "But the world won't let girls be kings. My envy and resentment are what you see. Not some… longing."

Jerrell raised her hand to his lips, kissed it.

She kept going, because Jerrell's misunderstanding needed to be cleared up. "And the professor… I'll show you my job congratulation letter from the White House. I had it before I ever slept with Dr. Messenger. That was just a one-time fling after a ball we both attended in my senior year. But he wanted to keep seeing me. I said no. I was getting ready to graduate and move on. To pursue me, he offered to make calls and get me a better position at the White House. He started contacting his buddies. His wife must've overheard and assumed I was screwing him so he would do me a favor. But I never needed him to, and I did… *not… ask.*"

Maddy sniffed back anguish and humiliation.

"I was wrong for sleeping with a married man. But I never needed him to—"

Jerrell's hand clawed her face, his thumb clipping her lips, silencing her.

He took a big breath. "Just give me a minute."

His hands, and his attention, shifted back to Maddy's waistline.

Concentrating, undeterred, he pulled down her bottoms. He hoisted her onto the sink counter, where she gripped the edges to balance herself.

When he placed his face at her valley, Maddy heard her juices hitting his tongue. Felt the nerves in her pussy canal coming alive again.

Her husband pushed his face inside her folds, while she clutched the back of his head. The meat of her thighs sat on his shoulders, feet dangling on his back, and bobbing while he pushed his tongue inside her. Slid it through her wetness. Reminded her she was a woman. Licked and slurped on Maddy like she was *his* woman.

Biting her bottom lip, this time when the tears two-stepped down her face, Maddy could only hold on. Jerrell's tongue attacked her creamy opening. After he lapped up her juice, he teased her exposed clit. Flipping her nub, he circled his tongue around it, and then dove back into her canal. Next, he slipped in his fingers. And tilted them up. Pressing the sweetest pressure point of her inner Christmas ornament.

Eyes crossed, her own tongue hanging, Maddy's body went limp. Her pussy pleaded for mercy. She was too scared to scream out the scorching sensations ringing in her womb. The baby still might be sleeping.

"Argh… mmph!" she shrieked, despite her best efforts at self-control.

Jerrell licked and lapped, head swaying, while his tongue sopped her up so hard, her hips rocked on his face. He finger-fucked and tongued her with reckless abandon, until the blizzard spun at her G-spot.

"Haaaaa…" she half-cried, half-begged. Jerrell didn't abort the mission until all of her had stopped snowing on his tongue, and he'd swallowed it all.

Like he was making a point, his face remained attached to Maddy's valley. His lips and tongue connected to every part of her he could.

Lifting her, he carried her back to the bedroom. With a peek at the crib, they saw that Chase still slept. They exchanged concerned stares of whether they should attempt the noise of sex that might wake him. But she hadn't felt her husband in months. Jerrell's expression said the same.

As they reached a silent agreement, she turned over and lay on her stomach, for their favorite position. He slid his arm under her flexible right leg and shifted it to her chest. She arched her back, pushed her butt up, anticipating the sweetest early Christmas gift. When he entered her, slipped inside, and his shaft tunneled up her wet, gurgling canal, they both almost climaxed immediately from the sheer pleasure of first contact.

His labored breathing filled her ear. A thick, commanding erection filled her to the hilt. Between exaggerated breaths, Jerrell murmured, "Whose pussy is this *now?*"

The very words, uttered while the tip of his wood beat the drum of her G spot, sent more of Maddy's cream dancing all over his dick. Her leg hoisted to her breast, he had more leverage, more access, so he could penetrate deeper.

"Urghhhh," she moaned.

Unable to keep her head up, her face plummeted into the pillow.

"I didn't hear you," he insisted, diving into her harder. His ax swung through her guts.

Chopped up all her Capitol Hill status, cut down that blustery ego, slashed through the country clubs and silly cliques.

Until it was just the two of them—him, and her pussy.

Too paralyzed while her eyeballs rolled to her brow bone, Maddy wasn't even part of the conversation.

From his crib, Chase woke up and started to whimper.

Maddy was too weak to speak.

Not breaking his stroke, Jerrell called out, "Hold on, son. I'm handling something. Daddy's coming." His dick attacked Maddy's insides that quaked, sending shockwaves through her core. She could hardly move to buck back. He repeated. "Madison?"

"Ergh… yours," she breathed into the pillow, her fists squeezing the pillowcase while her womanhood begged for mercy.

"*Say* it," he demanded, his balls slapping against her thighs.

At the sound of Jerrell's voice, with his dick pounding her relentlessly, Maddy's head snapped back. Santa rode Mommy's steaming hot sleigh to the North Pole.

"Aaah!" she screamed, bucking under the command of his rod beating her walls. "Daddy, it's yours!"

"Whose name is on this pussy?"

"J-Jerrell… hrrrgh… Rouse!" Maddy managed to reply while convulsing. "Urrrgh!"

Thrusting into her harder, she felt him shake. Felt his tortured breaths. He pumped a final time, groaning and shrieking out his ecstasy.

He only disconnected from her so she could feed Chase.

"Good girl." Jerrell slapped her ass. "*Now*, we're straight."

CHRISTMAS GIFTS

JERRELL, CHRISSY, SHELDON, DESMOND

JERRELL

"The baby doesn't like the Christmas tree looking that way," Maddy cracked.

Jerrell scoffed. "You mean his mama just wants to complain despite Daddy doing his damndest."

"Daddy could have used the white icicles I gave him, to add extra flare, and then it would be perfect," Maddy replied.

"Or Mommy could be grateful Daddy had energy to go get this big ass tree *she* picked out, and that he spent a whole day hauling it in here and putting it up. And she'll appreciate this tree and take these pictures," Jerrell noted, leaning over her and kissing her forehead.

He took a seat next to her on the sofa and threw his arm around her.

"Finally," their friend and photographer chimed in, pretending to wake up from a nap after hearing them go back and forth. "So, we're good now, folks?"

"I don't know. Maybe try asking the queen," Jerrell joked.

Maddy shifted Chase in her arms, so he was situated between them. "Come on, baby," she murmured to the little tot, who yawned like he was also tired of the fake arguing.

Jerrell leaned in. And slid his other arm underneath hers around their son. Before he could look to the camera, his eyes locked with his wife's. With the light of the tree spraying a soft haze around the room, and bouncing off their skin, she looked otherworldly. And she just might be.

From another world. As if the universe willed them, they gravitated to one another in a slow kiss.

"Thank you, Lord! He *does* have mercy on me," the photographer cried as, at last, they cooperated with the photoshoot.

The worlds spent inside Jerrell when he aligned with the two heavenly bodies next to him. On Earth, most folks called it kissing. But the way his prayers had been answered this time, it had to be so much more than that.

An hour later, they braved the New York City weather, to reach Santa's Workshop.

Chase was starting to fuss in Santa's arms.

"Here you go, baby! Smile! Chasey Poo… look at Mommy!" Maddy tried cajoling him.

Instead of smiling and gurgling the way he often did, the baby's face curled into an irritated scowl.

"Where's his pacifier?" Jerrell asked.

"He needs his Cuddle Bear. It's his favorite," Maddy said.

Jerrell searched through the diaper bag, starting to share Chase's frustration—he just wanted to go home. "Baby, where's *that*?"

"Left side pocket, J."

He kept scouring the bag. "It's not in here."

"Yes, it is. I packed it. You're not being thorough."

He stood up. "Forget it. I can make him laugh." Jerrell directed Maddy to take the baby and sit on Santa's leg. And then he sat on the other leg and smiled at his boy. "Hey, Handsome! Over here, dude, check it out," Jerrell cooed before sticking out his tongue. Immediately, his son's sleepy face spread into a smile and cracked up. "See? You can't make him smile like I can," Jerrell bragged with a half-cocked grin. He knew she wouldn't let that go unanswered.

As he predicted, Maddy sucked her teeth. "No, you just look funny."

Unbothered, Jerrell used his eyes as a whip, when he tossed her *that* look. "We'll see what's funny when we get home."

Her jaw fell slack.

From her silence, and no comeback, he saw she understood him clearly.

And even through her brick wall of a breastfeeding bra, her erect nipples poked out of her sweater like headlights.

Yeah, he knew how to shut her up too.

When all three were beaming, Santa's elf took the priceless shot.

CHRISSY

"Girl, stop fretting," Maddy fussed at Chriselle while clasping her bracelet around her wrist. "How do you move this much to be six months pregnant?"

On Christmas Eve, the emotional bride's arm jerked around, as it did when she had a performance. But when Chrissy's friends managed to distract her, she stared at the girlfriends she'd known practically since birth. "If you had asked me a year ago, would I ever marry again after escaping from Blake—"

"Girl," Maddy replied, "I would have slapped me *for* you."

Among the women laughing were Adella, and Chrissy's cousins, Neera and Cher. As well as two of Chrissy's other friends from high school and college.

"But you met a real man," Adella said.

"And after that baby is born, the only thing you'll be trying to escape are those morning knock-knocks," Maddy replied, her eyebrow cocked.

Chrissy chuckled, hitching her own eyebrow. "So, Jerrell's back to tearing that ass up, huh?"

Maddy's lips twisted around each other, and that was all the answer they needed. "More like nuclear annihilation."

Chrissy bathed in Maddy's glow; she was thrilled to see her friend happy again.

"You two are about to be sisters for real now," Neera pointed out.

Cher added, "Yeah, it's already bad enough we put up with you two in these streets, but now you're actually related. And Maddy will be here in New York. Watch out, world."

Staring at them all, Chrissy recalled the whirlwind year they'd had. "We're *all* sisters, already. We never needed men to cement that."

Adella nodded, raising her glass of cider. Her lips lifted in a smirk. "But still… watch out, world."

Chriselle fought back tears. This kind of joy hadn't looked possible a year ago, when Blake seemed to be holding up her entire life by her throat. Now, she raised her glass.

"That's right. The world really is ours," she murmured. "To us."

"To us," the others repeated.

Several insistent knocks on the door interrupted their girls' toast. "Mom! Uncle Jerrell said hurry up. He asked if he needs to come in here with a wheelbarrow and wheel you down the aisle!" Little Blake said from the other side of the door.

Chrissy stared at Maddy, whose shoulders started shaking. "*Your* husband."

SHELDON

Sheldon stared down the aisle at the angel coming toward him.

His brothers and a couple of cousins flanked his side.

Flashing through Shel's mind were the mistakes he'd made with his last choice of wife. With Genie, he'd moved too fast, and ignored the fatal flaws he'd seen in her. He'd been wrapped up in her streetwise sassiness and heart, without acknowledging that their very different upbringings and goals did not align.

Since Chrissy had disclosed to him what she did, he'd spent a lot of time checking in with himself.

He was now forty, and knew better this time around.

And Chrissy was still young, the mother of two impressionable, young children. With a third now on the way. They could not repeat their old mistakes.

And yet, Sheldon no longer harbored a single fear or doubt.

Genie would *never* have admitted to him what Chrissy had.

He knew that had taken rare courage.

He admired it.

Years ago, Chrissy had faced raising a son who was already too damaged by his father, a son who might have regressed even more if he saw his dad arrested. Back then, Chrissy still wasn't sure how she would survive if she made any sudden moves. So, she did turn a blind eye to her husband's money laundering and sex schemes and asked the young woman not to put him away, for a time. She'd kept her children stable, even if it meant taking a criminal risk.

But later, as she'd promised the young woman, Chriselle *did* handle Blake. Now he'd been convicted of RICO, and faced years of probation, in which he would be babysat by a judge.

A couple of months ago, after what Kevin Middleton had disclosed to Jerrell, who'd then shared it with him, the question had haunted Sheldon for weeks. He hadn't been terrified of what she'd done. He'd feared most that she would lie to him about it.

That would have been the end of them.

But his love had looked him squarely in his eye. The very same way she was looking at him now. And told him the truth.

Now those diamond-like eyes stared at him straight on,

unflinching, promising him she'd tell him the truth for a lifetime.

Admiring the woman she was, he kissed each one of her hands.

Surprising him, Chrissy lifted each of Sheldon's hands, laying her cheek in his palm when she kissed it. *Aahs* flowed around the church.

Her move sent his heart skipping atop the winter trees outside.

"Hi, baby," he whispered.

Chriselle's grin was both bashful and mischievous in the way that drove him nuts and kept his dick hard. "Hi, yourself."

DESMOND

A few weeks later, Desmond was toting out boxes Adella had labeled for the movers.

He and Del were packing up her Boston home and placing it on sale. They had purchased a loft in New York City and would stay at her family's home in Sag Harbor on weekends. Her grandparents' Cape Cod estate would continue being used primarily by Del's mother, aunts, uncles, and their children.

Although the city was lovely, Desmond had never grown attached to Boston. He was just fine with getting the hell away from the bulk of Del's relatives.

No disrespect.

In New York, he would be much closer to his hometown of Baltimore, a three-hour plane ride instead of seven. And he wouldn't be far from his boy Jerrell.

Plus, Keenan had given him an assistant manager role at *Slurp*, with the opportunity to buy into the *Explore* ownership and become a partner once he'd learned the ropes and proved himself.

It was a beginning. A stronger one than most former athletes received. He wouldn't spurn it. He knew his frustration at seeing Wes—or his anxiety about attending Hamptons parties—had nothing to do with Adella and was all about his own insecurities. And there was no question in Desmond's mind about her cheating or loving him. The only real issue wedged between them was his own sense of purpose and direction. Now he was addressing it.

After toting some boxes out to the driveway, he re-entered the house for a break.

The sight of Del standing atop the stairs froze him in his tracks.

She was coming down from their bedroom, and carrying some oblong object that might have been a toothbrush.

"I'm pretty sure I screwed the top back on the toothpaste this time," he said, trying to guess all the reasons she appeared dazed.

Her hand shot up. After peering a moment, he realized it wasn't a toothbrush.

But a pregnancy test.

He tried to get a read of her face, of whether this was

bad or good. If the tears glistening in her eyes were disbelief or disgust.

"Baby, it's okay. We'll keep tr—"

Del's smile broke through her lips and pressed against his mouth. As if contagious, her joy emanated into the core of him.

"Wait," he asked, still a little too shell-shocked to kiss her back. "We're having a…?"

His stunned, giddy wife nodded.

Whoooa.

The little tingles must've been excitement he felt exploding all over his body.

So, this was really happening. No turning back now. They were in this marriage for real.

Like… actual… grown up… adults.

With a tiny human for whom he was responsible.

Suddenly, he could no longer feel his heartbeat.

The room was turning black.

"Baby?" he heard Del call to him, from some distant point in space.

Desmond had passed out.

EPILOGUE

By the beginning of Black History Month, all the Black business-owners were finally present for a meeting of the Hamptons' Black Business Council. The photographer already had their seats lined up.

But first, they all greeted one another.

Adella came face-to-face with her childhood tormentor, Kevin Middleton.

He stuck out his hand. Mustering all the class her grandmother taught her, she accepted it and they shook.

No words.

When she moved to withdraw her hand, he held on. Adella and Kevin locked gazes again, and he studied her. As if throwing on a bulletproof vest, her mind prepared to respond to whatever verbal ammunition he was about to fire.

"You look lovely today, Adella. You wear marriage well." He released his grip.

She was unsure if her slight dizziness was morning sickness or disbelief. "Uh… thank you?"

Next to her was Maddy, who also shook his hand. "Kevin, I heard what you did for my husband and me a few weeks ago. We appreciate that."

Curtly, Kevin nodded. "The honor was mine. Glad you're here with us. I mean that."

Maddy and Del exchanged mystified expressions while moving around the social circle.

"Wow, is it possible Cher might be teaching him etiquette?" Adella asked.

"You know Cher keeps a whip, right?" Maddy joked under her breath.

Jerrell was up next in line. When he and Kevin shook hands, the grip remained for a moment, as if this greeting was genuine.

When Jerrell looked away, Maddy's gaze met her husband's. And their hands locked together. Jerrell licked his lips, slow. And the lips between her legs trembled, followed by a gush in her panties. Unable to suppress her grin, she chuckled at his cocky ass.

"What's wrong with you?" Adella asked. Then, Del caught the little exchange between Jerrell and Maddy. "Get out of here. You two are *not* doing that in public."

For the group photo, Maddy took her seat, and Jerrell assumed his spot standing behind her.

Sliding his hands over her shoulders, he watched his wife's body get all worked up, before he whispered, "Good girl."

THE END

(No, for real, it really is the end this time. I have a whole 'nother series to write!)

EXPLORE MEN OF THE HAMPTONS

THE SPIN-OFF SERIES TO SAG HARBOR

CAN THERE EVER BE HEALING IN THE HAMPTONS?

This novella was written right <u>after</u> the events in *Explore You*.

If you didn't read *Explore You*, and were kind of lost at certain points of this story, get your answers in this forbidden romance led by Kevin Middleton.

This is Book One of *Explore Men of the Hamptons*.

CHER

He starts coming toward me. His chest rises and falls.

I can't breathe. I'm not supposed to be doing this. It can't happen.

"Leave." I barely hear myself. Not through the scream of my brain, or tidal waves splashing through my veins, or the raging gallop of every nook and cranny within me.

He closes his eyes, shakes his head, while he backs me up against the wall. "No. Mm mm. Don't give me that weak crap. Say it like you mean it."

He opens those beautiful eyes again. His mouth dangles against mine.

And every fraction of every millisecond in which I say nothing is a moment I've waited too long.

Kevin half-whispers, half-breathes, "Chenera, tell me you don't want me, and I'll go."

Our cliques have hated each other since childhood…

What should Cher say?

THANKS FROM LULA

Thank you for reading *Rouse Family Christmas*! If you enjoyed this story, please leave a review at your favorite retailer.

If you were feeling the Rouse family and the characters in Sag Harbor, here's how you can stay connected.

Web site: www.lulawhitebooks.com

Email: lula@lulawhitebooks.com

Join Lula's Luxe Suite Reading Group:

http://www.facebook.com/groups/lulawhitelounge

Read the stories before they go on sale:

www.patreon.com/lulawhite

Lula's stories are available weeks to months in advance as she writes them on her Patreon. 🩶

Books In The *Sag Harbor Black Romances*
Brown Sugar This Christmas - Maddy & Jerrell
Hot Chocolate This Winter - Chrissy & Sheldon Part 1
Flinging All Spring - Adella & Desmond
Overheated for Summer - Chrissy & Sheldon Part 2
Rouse Family Christmas - All Couples

Books in the *Explore Men of the Hamptons* series

One Tasty Night - Solomon & Chaitra

Explore You - Kevin & Cher

Christmas Down Under - Keenan & Eugenia

Taste You - Solomon & Chaitra

Drink You - Lion & Kamila

See Through You - Keenan & Eugenia

Find You - Roland & Neeraja